THE MOB

THE MOB

JUDGE, JURY, & EXECUTIONER™ BOOK EIGHTEEN

CRAIG MARTELLE

MICHAEL ANDERLE

LMBPN

DISRUPTIVE IMAGINATION

Version 1.01, February 2023
ebook ISBN: 979-8-88878-018-3
Print ISBN: 979-8-88878-019-0

THE MOB TEAM

Thanks to our Beta Readers

In memoriam, Micky Cocker, James Caplan, Kelly
O'Donnell, and John Ashmore

Thanks to the JIT Readers

Daryl McDaniel
Dave Hicks
Veronica Stephan-Miller
Diane L. Smith
James Caplan
Jackey Hankard-Brodie
Rachel Beckford
Peter Manis
John Ashmore
Kelly O'Donnell
Zacc Pelter
Jeff Goode
Jan Hunnicutt

Editor
Lynne Stiegler

We can't write without those who support us
On the home front, we thank you for being there for us

We wouldn't be able to do this for a living if it weren't for our
readers
We thank you for reading our books

CHAPTER ONE

Heavy Frigate _Wyatt Earp_, Interstellar Space

"Eat me!" Red's face boiled with his fury. "Eat me, you sock-fucking, crusty, hair-infested asshole! Fuck you! Fuck you right in your glass eyeball."

Rivka's mouth fell open as she stared in disbelief.

Tyler stood behind her in the corridor, a towel over his shoulder.

Red hammered on the door with his massive fist. "I'll break your ass. Rip you right the fuck in half."

"I'll be in our quarters," Tyler said. He strolled down the corridor.

Heavy steps pounded on the deck plates. Three hard chargers bolted into the corridor from the cargo bay. "Fight!"

"No, no fight," Rivka said.

"We heard someone giving the high hard one. There has to be a fight." Furny, one of the three newest members of the crew, was confused. Rivka had put the newcomers under Alant Cole's command. _Wyatt Earp_ now had its own squad of armor-clad warriors. All it took was the overactive libidos of her three young pilots and the subterfuge of the entire crew in hiding them after they came aboard until they were a long way from *War Axe*.

Cole stepped out after his team. "It's just Red. He usually yells like that. Pay it no mind. Now get back in here. We're not done." Cole returned through the airlock to the cargo bay.

Furny, Lewis, and Russell stood their ground. "There has to be a fight."

"He's mad because the door won't open," Rivka explained. She stood in her workout gear, untainted by dirt or sweat because no one had been able to get into the gym. Clevarious was keeping it locked.

"Open up, you piece of slime-infested runny dogshit!" Red continued to beat on the door.

"I'm out." Rivka threw her hands up and returned to her quarters.

"C, honey, could you help us out here? Working out is important to us. I mean, really important. We have to be finely tuned if we're to protect Rivka," Lindy said with a smile.

Floyd trundled down the corridor, running into each of the warriors' legs, bouncing off them in play as she continued to Red and Lindy. Der'ayd'nil, Red and Lindy's son, flew casually after the wombat.

His mother held out her arm for him to land. "Can you ask Clevarious why he's being intransigent?"

Dery laughed and hugged Lindy's neck. He spoke into his parents' minds, *He knows what you do not.*

As usual, they had no idea what their son meant.

"Can you explain a little more? How does knowing what we don't translate into locking us out of the gym? Is there a monster in there?" Red shrugged. He couldn't imagine what it might be.

Patience leads to revelation. The boy flew away. Floyd ran after him.

"I guess that's it. We're not working out today. We're left with 'all things will be clear' at some nebulous point in the future."

"Your son is weird," Furny muttered as he watched the boy flutter toward the bridge.

A sound that was little more than a whisper on the wind was the only warning the warrior received before Red had him by the throat and pinned against the wall. "You watch your fucking mouth. That boy saved this crew and this ship multiple times already. You haven't been on the ship long enough to know that we're all weird, and weird is good.

"If you mean it in a bad way, I'll beat you so bad your grandkids have bruises. Then I'll pound them, too, just because you fucked with the wrong guy."

Lindy leaned against her husband. "If you're not weird on this crew, you're not trying. You'll get your chance to prove yourself soon enough. Until then, I suggest you keep your opinions to yourselves.

"If you have a question, ask Cole. He gets it. We all have a role to play. This business is far too dangerous to have any conflict among the crew, so let me add one more suggestion. Try to fit in by being appropriately weird."

Red let him down.

"How fucking strong *are* you?" Furny asked. "I'm no one's lightweight."

"We work out every day, and we have a Pod-doc." Red winked. "Be weird, my man."

"Ryleigh never said we'd get beaten up. We're going to have words."

Red took two steps and stopped. "Those three are our little sisters. Don't hurt them, and we won't have any problems."

Lewis raised his hand. Red and Lindy looked at each other and turned back to the fresh meat. "Yes?"

"Are we slaves?"

"You're members of *Wyatt Earp's* crew and teammates of Magistrate Rivka Anoa. She calls the shots, and you'll do her bidding, or you'll be off at the next planet. If you stick with us, you'll find that there is no greater satisfaction in the universe than supporting her and what she does—bringing Justice to the downtrodden so all can live in peace. It's a higher calling. No. You're not slaves except to your own consciences. You wouldn't be here if Terry Henry thought you were lacking."

A voice called from the cargo bay, "Stop fucking off and get in here!"

The three new additions scurried away.

"You think you might have been a little hard on him?" Lindy asked.

"No one gives shit to our son."

"He is different, but I would never say weird. *You're* weird." Lindy wrapped her arms around her husband. "Weirdly righteous!"

"That's what I like to hear. Didn't we get some new

weapons from the Bad Company when we were hooked up to the *War Axe*?" Red knew the answer. He had been the one running like a kid at Christmas after Kai stuffed a bunch of developmental toys into his arms.

"So I hear." Lindy casually walked away. She took off her workout shirt and tossed it into the air behind her.

Red caught it and looked around to make sure no one else was in the area. "Hey! Someone could see you."

"The other men are all in the cargo bay or in Rivka's quarters. Remember when we used to be young and free? Are you getting old?"

"What? What the hell? Them's fightin' words."

She removed her bra, threw it behind her, and ran.

"Are they gone?" Rivka asked.

"Yes, Magistrate. You can use the workout room now," Clevarious replied.

"You have not yet explained why you aren't letting them work out. I find myself at a loss as to what the explanation could be." Rivka waited for a moment before leaving her quarters with Tyler on her heels.

Your next case, C said, using her communication chip for maximum privacy.

You always know before I do. I stopped letting that upset me. As long as someone knows, we're all good, and the universe will not collapse under the weight of the unknown. So, what don't I know?

You'll be going undercover to infiltrate the mob.

I'm not sure I like the sound of that. So why can't Red work out?

Because you'll be going in with Atticus Tikabow and no one else.

Rivka stood before the gym door, and it opened for her, but she didn't enter. "Custer? Why am I being partnered with him? And why can't Red work out? Spill it, bitch!" Rivka turned around and ran into Tyler.

"I guess we're going back to the room?"

"Just me. You work out. You'll need to have your best game for later." She winked at him, but her expression was dark. It suggested she would be calling Grainger and ripping him a new butthole. Tyler stepped out of the way. He knew that look only too well.

"Your wish is my command," he replied and swatted her backside.

She chuckled while pointing at him. "You're heading the right way, mister!" She continued to her quarters, and Tyler surrendered to the inevitability of the impending chaos.

Clevarious continued when the Magistrate was alone in her quarters. "You know Red. We know Red. We don't want him to get hurt. In that vein, everyone out there knows Red. He needs to not look like Red. To do that, we're going to shrink him a bit in the Pod-doc."

Rivka snorted. "Does Red know this?"

"Not yet, Magistrate. He might be resistant. We were thinking of drugging him."

Rivka sat at her desk and brought up the hologrid. "Wait a minute. You said I was going alone with Custer. How does Red figure into this?"

"Do you think Red would let you go anywhere without him?"

Rivka shook her head. "You're one step ahead of me. Well, probably five steps, but you're right. So, Red is going in under double cover because if Grainger found out, he'd birth a bistok. So Red can't look like Red."

"He can't act like Red, either." Clevarious sounded less confident.

Rivka snorted again. "We'll have to do our best. So you'll drug him, shrink him, and then ask that he not act like himself so he can be exactly what he is—my body-guard, who cannot be bested in single combat by any criminal."

"Something like that," Clevarious agreed.

Rivka scrolled through the holoscreens, looking for Grainger's orders. She found them, listed as "Low Priority" so they wouldn't appear in her feed. They had been sent twelve minutes earlier.

The AIs already had a plan for the execution of the case.

"Connect me to Grainger, please." Rivka leaned back and crossed her arms. She glared at the screen.

"There you are! Happy-happy, joy-joy. May your bless-ings be bountiful and your orgasms be plentiful. How can I help you on this fine day, Rivka?"

Rivka didn't flinch. She stared unblinking at the screen. She'd improved her abilities after trying to stare down the Crenellian Ankh, which she had yet to do successfully. However, the practice made her an indomitable force among her fellow humans.

"You saw the new case, huh?" Grainger continued.

"You're teaming me with a stranger to penetrate the

mob? Why do we have to do it that way? Why not the old way of shoving a warrant in their ugly faces while we charge in to secure the evidence of their many crimes?"

"If it were only so straightforward. This isn't like any mob you've seen before. I'm not even sure we can classify them as the mob because first and foremost, we don't know who's in charge. We don't know where their home planet is, and we don't know how they run their business. All we know is that drugs are moving around the galaxy, and all the signs point to a centralized control. That's where things break down because all the signs are pointing in different directions."

Rivka tried to parse Grainger's words, as she usually did when he said something he thought was profound when it was simply a jumble of words. She decided it was time to turn his tactic around and give him a taste of it.

"It's decentralized centralized control to deliver maximum dispersion through a single focal point that's not a single point at all. It's genius."

"Clearly, you're the right person for the case. I've asked a civilian lawyer who has defended some slimy personalities and has access to the underworld, as it may be. You know him. Atticus Tikabow."

She maintained a neutral expression, which she wouldn't have been able to do had she heard his name for the first time from Grainger.

"What kind of undercover work do you think we'll be doing?"

"You'll have to pose as his girlfriend." Grainger leaned toward the screen to be as intimidating as he could.

Rivka leaned close too and spoke slowly to make her

point. "Fuck that. I'll pose as his new boss who wants a piece of the action. If you make any more noise about a girlfriend, I'll be on my way to wherever you are and send *you* out there as Custer's girlfriend. Do I make myself crystal-clear?"

Grainger backed away from the screen and canted his head. "There used to be a time when I was in charge."

"Undercover work has to be voluntary. You know that. You also believe that the word 'volunteer' does not have to be preceded by the word 'I.' On that point, I disagree. Those are my conditions, or find yourself a different pillow monkey to do your bidding."

"Jael already turned me down."

"Clevarious, send a box of chocolates and a dozen roses to Jael from a secret admirer who thinks she is intelligent and witty and the only thing lacking in her life is a good man."

"Of course," the SI replied aloud so Grainger could hear.

The ship was idled while they took downtime after the last case. The stink of Nefas had infected the morale of the ship, and everyone was just starting to lighten up. Rushing into another case was what they did every time.

Rivka was getting tired of it. "We need a few more days, Grainger. This pace isn't healthy. Someone is going to get hurt, most likely Custer, if you send me in there right now."

"No problem at all. Report to these coordinates tomorrow. Interstellar space before continuing to Blue Heron Four, where you'll liaise with Barrister Tikabow's contact." A series of numbers popped up on the screen. Rivka ignored them, knowing Clevarious had logged them into the navigation system.

"I already suspect Custer's dirty, so you're not throwing that twist my way."

"We don't think he is. Just blinded by the massive number of credits building in his accounts. He can be bought, but he isn't anti-Federation. He definitely isn't anti-Rivka."

"What makes you say that? I expect I'm going to dread your answer."

"See? You don't need to touch anyone to see their deep dark secrets. He has been drinking lately and lamenting the one who got away."

"For fuck's sake, Grainger. And you want to put me with this guy for a few days? I'm married by every standard in the galaxy. I'm not going to hang with a lovelorn Custer."

"Did you go before a judge? No? Then you're not married. And for your information, this is going to take some time. You'll be his boss, so you can treat him like dirt. Set him on a new path of loathing."

"For fuck's sake, Grainger!" Rivka repeated. Grainger seemed disconnected from the reality of the situation. "He'll love me that much more if I stomp a spiked heel in the middle of his chest. You're going to owe me for this one, and it's probably going to cost you something with Tyler, too."

"I'll send you chocolates and roses. I think I'll have some extra ones lying around here pretty soon."

CHAPTER TWO

<u>Baron's Hold, Blue Heron Four</u>

Asheka Burako, Ash, had his back to the newcomer. He looked out the small window of a fourth-story flat in the less-desirable Baron's Hold district at the bustling city beyond. It used to be home to slaves and other indentured servants. It was out of the limelight.

That was the most desirable trait for Ash's workspace.

There were no electronics in the place. It operated manually because slaves deserved no modern conveniences. Upgrades cost money, and upgrades invited technicians into where they weren't wanted.

Since Ash had no trustworthy techs in his employ on Blue Heron Four, he did without.

That meant a parade of individuals—human, Yollin, and every flavor in between—because he still needed to manage the business of feeding sordid appetites throughout this sector of the galaxy and beyond. He was important, at least in his own mind.

A hulking six-legged alien blocked the door from the outside, making no secret of the presence of someone who mattered. Law enforcement never came into the Hold's block housing. It was far too dangerous, and no one in the blocks would cooperate. They'd be as good as dead if anyone thought they were a snitch.

It was the way of life in the blocks. Too many knew nothing else. They lived and they died just trying to get by. They had nowhere else to go, and even if they did, they had no credits to get them there.

"Hex! Send in the next victim."

Sheven Eskatch came from a rare race of sentient beings called Atchimorians. Had he not been sentient, he would have been on some planet's endangered species list, protected by keeping him in a zoo. Hex was much more useful than that. He was the muscle who kept the applicants and informants in check.

"You," Hex's bold bass bellowed. "Come."

"Yes, sir, Bug Legs," a snappy and irreverent voice shouted back.

"Ass," the Atchimorian rumbled. "As in, suck my."

The scuffle in the hallway delayed the arrival of the next applicant. The door pushed open the rest of the way, and a Crenellian wearing a big smile and a reddening bruise on the side of his face entered.

"Did you think taunting the Atchimorian was a good idea?"

"Is that what he is? Weird. I thought he was some mutant Yollin. A genetic experiment gone madly awry. Bug Legs seems kind of angry."

"It's a learned trait. Why are you here?" Ash asked. He crossed his arms and mentally gave the small creature ten seconds to make an impression.

"I'm Crenellian," he started.

"You're wasting my time by telling me what I already know."

"What you don't know is that I'm not a normal Crenellian. Their emotionless bullshit isn't for me. You see, I can do the math, but I can have fun with it, too. Like, millions of hits on transports around the system. Hits you want delivered and to be compensated for. Who's willing to pay the most, and how do we put that amount in the right supplier's hands? Am I right?"

"You're annoying is what you are. You've exceeded your ten seconds to make a good impression. Get out."

"Delegor. Voracious appetite for Plexorall and Advantageous. A shipment was recently confiscated by local law enforcement at the behest of a Magistrate. I know how to keep the Magistrates away from your operation."

"You have my attention, but you don't have my respect. You strike me as a little weasel. I doubt I'll ever trust you, and that is a dangerous way to live your life." Ash held up his finger to forestall the Crenellian from continuing. "I don't know who the Magistrates are. Is that another one of your ploys?"

Ash knew about the Magistrates, but he had wanted to hear the Crenellian's take on them.

"I don't care if you don't trust me. Few do at first, but in the end, I'll earn your trust. I'll do what I say I'm going to do. For your information, the Magistrates are the single most destructive unit from the Federation's judicial branch. They operate outside the law with the Queen's blessing. It's a Reynolds conspiracy to control every aspect of our lives."

"I don't feel controlled." Ash surveyed the world before him. Slums. The blocks. It didn't seem to be controlled by anyone but those who lived there. It was little more than anarchy. "The Magistrates. Tell me your plan and be quick about it."

"My plan is the only leverage I have. If I walk out of here without a deal, that Yollin misfit, Mister Bug-Legged Bastard, will tear me in half. I need some kind of guarantee."

"If you don't tell me, I'll kill you myself. If you run, Hex will kill you. If you tell me and I don't like it, Hex will kill you. That leaves you no options. Impress me and live." Ash uncrossed his arms, interlaced his fingers, and cracked his knuckles. He stood with his arms loose at his sides. Ash was done with the verbal jousting. He stared at the Crenellian, counting down from five. If he reached zero before the miscreant spoke, he'd break the weasel's skinny neck. Hex would take care of the body. He'd gotten rather good at it.

The Crenellian must have sensed that his time for word play was at an end.

"We give them something juicier as bait."

Ash rolled his finger. The interview was coming to an end.

"We give them Tommy 'Silver Tongue' Gamble."

"Never heard of her." Ash crossed his arms again. He

looked at the ceiling. Patience wasn't his virtue. He had to admit it was a vice since he had none.

"Because he doesn't exist. I've already put out feelers regarding funneling sales data through his estate and that the front-line dealers would be getting their orders from him."

"This is a dangerous game you're playing."

"I wouldn't be here if I wanted to pull this off. I'd do it behind your back, hiding every move I made. I *am* hiding my moves, but I'm not doing it to horn in on your action. I'm doing it to support you and build your empire."

"That's where you're mistaken, Crenellian. I have no empire. No one does because there's no single individual in charge."

"That's irrelevant to what I'm doing. What I'm doing is decoying the Magistrates. They like going after big fish. Have you seen their conviction record?"

Ash turned his back on the Crenellian, having deemed him physically harmless. Had he been carrying a weapon, Hex would have known and prevented him from entering.

"What's your name, Tiny?"

"You can call me 'Tiny.' That works." The Crenellian bobbed his big head until he started to sway. He stopped to keep from falling over.

Ash struck like a cobra. He caught the small being by the neck and lifted. "Enough games, you little piece of shit. I asked your name."

"I am Bint'An'Tool. You can call me Tiny," the Crenellian wheezed. His small hands gripped Ash's forearms. He choked out, "Nice cannons."

"I refer to them as howitzers," Ash replied. He relaxed

his grip. "'Tiny' is too good for you. You'll be 'Bent Anus,' or 'Anus' for short."

"I can go by Amos."

"Well, Anus, what kind of guarantee can you give me that the Magistrates will be distracted? I could use that sooner rather than later."

"We have to start slowly. You know the sentient intelligence life forms are working with them, right? We only have to hint about Tommy 'Silver Tongue' Gamble on open channels with some order information. We'll use real orders, so someone will have to be sacrificed. I recommend those idiots on Delegor."

"They deserve what they get. If they can help us along the way, so be it. Who on Delegor do you have in mind? I still don't trust you, for reference, but you know a lot more than you should. Coming in here like this was high risk."

"But high-reward. I have the utmost confidence in myself."

"That makes one of you," Ash replied. "I'll most likely terminate our relationship through your death, but until then, you can consider it to be high-reward. Then one day, you can aspire to digs like these. Look at this view!" He spread his arms to take in the crumbling refuge containing the worst Blue Heron Four had to offer.

"You and I both know you don't live here." The Crenellian knew too much. Ash considered killing him for that alone, but since Smiley O'Keefe got condemned to Jhiordaan, he'd needed a deputy. Hex wasn't that person. He enjoyed the wet work too much. He had less patience than Ash. Bodyguard and muscle was the perfect role.

Mutant Yollin. Ash smiled at the plastisheet window.

The tiny asshole wasn't too far off. He was growing on him.

"Introduce Silver Tongue to the universe. I think he needs to covertly travel to Delegor sometime in the next three days. We have a huge shipment headed to Black Spruce. I'd like it to get there."

"Where's Black Spruce?" Bint asked.

"It's nowhere near Delegor. That's all you need to know, you little fuck. Plant the seed, water it, and let's see how it grows. If you're going to join the Burako clan, you need to earn my trust." Ash waved his hand.

Bint'An'Tool was dismissed. He decided it wasn't in his best interests to push any further. He'd made as much progress as he had anticipated and possibly more.

He dipped his head briefly and strolled out the door, refusing to show fear.

Ash and Hex had to respect that. The Crenellians were one of the least physically intimidating races in the galaxy. They had to know that since they were also one of the most intelligent. But Ash had never heard of one who was *emotionally* intelligent. That concerned him. After the Crenellian was gone, he summoned Hex.

"Put one of your boys on him. He knows too much, which tells me he might be an undercover operative. We need to milk him for all he's worth and then do him."

"I'll do him right now, bossman. Just say the word. I already put a tail on him. There was no way I was letting that one get away, not with everything I heard. Sorry, bossman. I always listen whenever someone's with you. I don't want any surprises. I'm too old to go work for someone else. I don't have enough life left to break in another like you."

"I guess that's one way to look at it. Thanks, Hex. You're a good man. You have to admit the mutated Yollin part was kind of funny."

"Yollins are candy-asses. I haven't met one that can take me yet. So no, I don't have to admit it was funny. Are you calling me a candy-ass?"

"Just an ass. No candy to it, Hex."

The smile on the Atchimorian's face disappeared. "Hey!"

"Is there anyone else out there?" Ash nodded at the hallway outside the flat.

Hex shook his head.

"Let's call it a day. I see a game of hackball in my future. Join me?"

"Hackball? Are you using the stuff you're selling?"

Ash clapped the oversized creature on the shoulder. "You know the golden rule. Nobody in the chain uses. Otherwise, they find themselves dancing on the bottom of the deep blue sea. Blue Heron isn't called blue because of our music."

"You got that right, boss man. I shan't be joining you because I have some self-respect. Chasing a little ball around eighteen finely-manicured lawns? Sounds like torture."

"It is, but the good kind. Bring the car around."

"Already on its way." Hex had a comm chip and used it to stay one step ahead of Asheka Burako. Ash wasn't enamored of having technology so close to him, but he hadn't heard of an instance where a chip had been hacked to reveal the location of its user.

Then again, he wasn't up on everything the Singularity was capable of. That was why Tommy "Silver Tongue" Gamble was going to play a key role in keeping the focus away from the Burako clan.

CHAPTER THREE

<u>Interstellar Space beyond Blue Heron Four</u>

"Custer," Rivka said.

"Is that any way to greet your old flame? The light of your life?" The barrister was tall and lean, with a quick smile and sparkling eyes. He was easy to look at, but deep down, he had a competitive streak that had sent Rivka running for the exit. In his mind, she was the light of his life. In hers, he was a good-looking mistake.

He zoomed in for a hug. She stiff-armed him in the chest. She caught a glimpse of what was in his mind, but not enough to solidify his thoughts. "I'm not here of my own accord. I'm perfectly happy having nothing to do with you."

He put his hands on his hips and pouted. "After all this time, absence didn't make the heart grow fonder? Come on! Admit that you still think about me."

"I don't think about you, not in the least. After you won the case of the guilty murderer, I found my way into the

Magistrate Corps. This is a much better fit for me than being a simple barrister."

She didn't know why she threw that last part in. Maybe it was a feeble attempt to get under his skin. Probably. She wanted to wipe that perpetual smirk off his face. She also didn't want to touch him and get a clearer picture of his thoughts.

"You shot down the girlfriend angle, I heard. Boss will work, but new boss. I've defended a number of these guys in court. Only lost the last case because the guy was an idiot. He made his hits in the open with too many witnesses and in sight of a high-resolution camera. He had no chance, but the jury has mercy. They gave him Jhiordaan instead of the death penalty. The mob didn't hold it against me."

"We'll call that something of a win. Where are we headed, and who are we meeting?" Rivka crossed her arms and tucked her hands into her armpits.

"Blue Heron Four, to the block called Baron's Hold to meet with Ash Burako. He's a player, but small-time. He'd like to be big-time, but he's not savvy enough for that. It was his deputy that got sent to Jhiordaan." Atticus continued wearing his annoying smile as if he'd just delivered the best news ever.

"Is that it?"

"Gotta start somewhere, Riv." Custer looked down the corridor while the airlock cycled and the ship that had delivered him disconnected.

"Is that all you have?" One small bag sat in the airlock.

"We're in a hurry, so I didn't have time to pack. We need

to look the part, your highness." Rivka walked away. "Aren't you going to introduce me to your crew?"

"You're not going to be here that long. Once we let the mob kill you, I'll arrest the perpetrators. You can go to your grave, comfortable in the knowledge that I will make them pay with a good six months to a year in the local prison for their crime."

"Very funny. Why the hostility? You wouldn't be a Magistrate if I hadn't won that case that triggered whatever is inside of you. You're welcome."

Rivka's eye twitched. She wasn't sure what she was feeling, but it wasn't anything special for Atticus Tikabow. He was just a guy she used to know, a relic of her distant past. She'd have to talk to Tyler about it. She couldn't be that hostile toward him while they were undercover. Or maybe she could. What would it take to earn the mob's trust? Probably not the friendly approach.

"Get used to it. This is how your new superior is going to treat you. We'll be far more believable if we're not buddy-buddy."

Tyler leaned against the hatch leading to the bridge. He held Floyd in his arms, a ploy to avoid shaking hands or getting too close to someone. Rivka felt instant jealousy that she hadn't thought of it. Floyd was quite a load and created a fair amount of stand-off distance.

"Magistrate," Kennedy called from the flight deck. "We have an issue. A transport is approaching."

"This is interstellar space. There's no reason for a ship to be out here. There's no Gate anywhere near." As she eased past Tyler, she grabbed him and planted a passionate kiss on his mouth.

Me, too! Floyd cried.

Rivka kissed the wombat on the top of her head, then entered the bridge and jumped into the captain's chair. "Move us toward them, but under no circumstances are we to make contact. Squawk us something that's not tied to Magistrate Rivka Anoa. Make a high-speed pass. See if we can intimidate them."

Kennedy accelerated *Wyatt Earp* toward the transport.

"Squawking *Terribellus*, a pirate ship we destroyed."

"Pirates. That works." Rivka rubbed her chin as the transport grew bigger on the screen.

"They are attempting to warn us off."

"Let them wonder. Continue accelerating. Clear them by a hundred meters. That's plenty of cushion." Rivka leaned back and watched.

A hundred meters was not much of a cushion, not when one spaceship was trying to avoid another. Kennedy adjusted rapidly, countering the transport as quickly as they could maneuver. They stopped trying after a minute and adopted a steady course. *Wyatt Earp* ripped past.

"Maintain course to Blue Heron Four."

"Cloak us?"

"No. That'll beg more questions than it avoids. Once they saw us, that's all she wrote. In any case, continue squawking *Terribellus* and get us in the landing pattern. We'll stay outside the main city of Baron's Hold." She watched the crew work until a hand touched her shoulder.

She almost came out of her skin.

It was Atticus, and Tyler was standing next to him.

"Doctor Tyler Toofakre, my husband. He'll kick your ass if you touch me again."

Tyler snorted. Rivka had made it abundantly clear that she wasn't to be fought over like some prize at a bistok-busting contest.

The crew on the bridge looked at each other in confusion.

"I'll do it!" a voice bellowed from the corridor.

"That's my bodyguard, Vered the Mighty. We call him Red. His wife Lindy is back there, too. Ryleigh and Kennedy are at the controls. Clodagh is around here some-where. Listen for a little dog yapping. We have Three SCAMPs, a Crenellian, the Embassy of the Singularity, a squad of Bad Company warriors, and two little kids, one of whom has wings and flies around the ship. This is Floyd, our little girl. She's a wombat."

Atticus was ill-prepared for the menagerie that consti-tuted Rivka's crew. "Great to meet all of you." His discom-fort brought Rivka unexpected joy. He marshaled his strength and continued, "I have some information that I need to brief you on when we can."

"I'll assemble my team in the conference room," Rivka replied.

"No team. This is just for you." He shook his head.

Rivka rotated the captain's chair to look at him. Behind Atticus, Red scowled. His mouth worked. "Fuck that. I'm coming, too."

"You're not coming," the lawyer stated and waved dismissively. Red reached for him, but Rivka raised her hand. Atticus looked behind him to find Red's massive arm dangerously close. He flinched and ducked out of the way. "Is this how you do things? Your answer to everything is violence?"

Rivka put on her sweetest smile. She had gotten under his skin. "When it's your job to put dangerous criminals out of business, one must be more dangerous. Yes. We solve a great number of issues with abject violence, but it's controlled. We apply the right level to each situation, but most of the time, the perps give us no choice, and we have to kill them. As a Magistrate, I don't have to deal with people like you. Your clients better be happy that they don't have to deal with me since there is no defense counsel and there is no appeal."

He recoiled in horror. "Is that what you do? That's not how our justice system works. It's illegal. You're nothing more than an assassin." He shuffled his feet as if he were trying to escape the bridge. Red blocked him, crossing his arms and swelling to his full size. Tyler moved to the side and leaned against the bulkhead. Floyd was snoring, nothing but dead weight.

"I think the proper terminology is 'Judge, Jury, and Executioner.' It's not a job for the meek or the weak or the likes of you. That's probably why I'm here. There's a hard job ahead of us that only one of us is authorized to do."

"Authorized!" Atticus appeared to be growing a spine. It was best to get any consternation out in the open before they went in to meet his contact. Atticus would be sufficiently cowed when he finally understood what Rivka really did as a purveyor of Justice.

She had already murdered one of his clients. Although that hadn't been intentional, it had been the right outcome. He had been found innocent by a jury, but he was a killer, and he would have killed again. His death had saved lives, and that was the end of it.

The deaths of all of those she convicted would save lives.

"Shut up and listen," she told him. "The Magistrates operate under the authorization of the signatories to the Federation Charter. We were hauled before them to answer for what we did. We were cleared and turned loose to go back to work—the work of keeping the likes of your clients out of the lives of the common citizen. We know beyond a shadow of a doubt that they're guilty before we mete out punishment, up to and including death."

"The citizens of the Federation are entitled to a trial by a jury of their peers. They are not to be judged by single individuals with no right of appeal. You murdered my client, who was found not guilty!"

Rivka surged out of her seat. "He was guilty as sin, and you knew it. Getting him off was the crime. Lawyers and politicians built the framework within which decent society works so people can go to work in the morning and feel secure in what they're doing. They should never fear for their safety, whether it's physical safety, emotional safety, or financial safety. Your clients disrupt all three and benefit from the flaws in the system that you exploit."

Rivka returned to her seat after her spit-flecked tirade. "If you want to finish this case with any semblance of your dignity intact, you'll change your view of those you seek to represent. You've sold your soul for a few credits and a so-called glamorous lifestyle. It's all smoke and mirrors. In the end, you have nothing but what you are inside."

Red loomed over him.

"I still need to brief you," he said in a small voice.

"Me and my team, of course, even though they won't be with us," Rivka clarified.

Red reiterated his previous point. "Fuck that. I'm coming along."

"You are not," Rivka replied. She winked at him, knowing Clevarious and the others had a plan. He looked ready to explode. Rivka got up and nudged him out of the way.

"If only you weren't so big," she mumbled as she passed. Lindy smiled at her from the corridor.

Sleep! Floyd whined when Tyler tried to put her down. He waddled after Rivka, still carrying the wombat.

"Come on, little man. You're starting to get a clue as to how things are done." Red wrapped his arm over Custer's shoulders. The lawyer tried to shrug it off, but the body-guard wasn't letting go.

C, I can know nothing about what you're doing to Red and with Red. Just make it happen. I'll feel a lot better if he's close by while I'm down there or anywhere this lead takes us.

Of course. The Singularity is looking into new information. There might be a new head of the organization, a Tommy Gamble. There is very little on him. We will keep digging.

You guys are always one step ahead of us. Have something to share at the briefing that'll start in a couple minutes. Have Chaz and Dennicron join us, along with Clodagh, please.

Rivka casually strolled to her conference room. Inside, she took her usual seat. She pointed at the chair in which she wanted Custer to sit, which was as far away from her as possible.

Tyler joined them and carefully put Floyd on the table. She snuffled but didn't wake up. "I'll be right back." Red and Lindy took their seats. Rivka held up one finger to make Custer wait to start the briefing.

Chaz and Dennicron joined them. Both were running their series of bubbly subroutines. They beamed at Custer and introduced themselves.

"Self-Contained Artificial Mobility Platforms. SCAMPs. They are SIs who have the ability to move around. Clevarious runs the ship. Erasmus and Ankh have a wife, Chrysanthemum. She's running around here somewhere in a SCAMP body as well. You can call her 'Mrs. Ambassador.'"

Tyler returned with a pillow that he wedged around Floyd's body, with a corner of it under her head.

"Is that my pillow?"

Tyler shrugged. "Maybe."

"I never took you for the marrying type," Custer said.

Rivka stared at him until the tension ratcheted up to a level the Magistrate found appropriate. "You can start your briefing."

CHAPTER FOUR

<u>Blue Heron Four, Landing Field Epsilon 17</u>

"Custer? It's time to go ashore."

The lawyer looked at her. He wanted to say something, but Rivka couldn't tell what. Was he going to start arguing again?

"Why is it ashore? The oceans are not near here. This isn't a shore. I thought you militant types called it dirtside or something inane like that."

"Dirtside is for grunts. We're more cultured here, like the Marines, because that's what Terry Henry was. He says ashore. We're saying ashore. And 'militant' and 'military' are two very different things. You know that.

"Don't be an asshole this whole trip. If you get me killed, I can guarantee my crew will come after you, and you will suffer greatly. I won't be here to stop them. See, unlike your compatriots, mine are loyal because they want to be, not because they are afraid or because they are paid. To this day, I don't know what any of us are getting paid, and that includes me."

Custer half-smiled. "You don't know what you get paid? How is that possible?"

"Because I have everything I need and then some. You should think about the people you surround yourself with and not the façade that you've built."

Custer smiled. "You used to be a damn good lawyer, but now you're different. A leader with a crew that adores you. No one dares cross you." He looked at the deck as he kicked at it with one toe. "I'm envious. I make a lot of credits. I can do whatever I want, just until they call with another case."

"That part sounds like me. I wasn't given a choice in this case either."

"Mission," Red grumbled from the corridor. He pushed off the bulkhead and walked away. The Magistrate and the lawyer watched him go.

"Would he have beat me up?"

"Who says he still won't?" Rivka raised one eyebrow.

Custer threw up his hands in surrender. "I concede the case, Barrister. We plead guilty on all counts. I throw myself on the mercy of the court."

Rivka dipped her chin before turning serious. "Keep your wits about you, Custer. These are bad people. There's no posturing and no playing. Every interaction is for all the cards. Every single one. Don't let your guard down."

"I work with these people, and this one especially. I'm aware of who and what they are. Can you deal with them without resorting to violence?"

Rivka snorted, but the sound came from deep in her throat. "I have people to impart violence." She waved toward the cargo bay on the other side of the ship. "I have a squad of power-armored warriors. They can level a small city, and if you include the firepower that *Wyatt Earp* carries, we can level a large city. I don't take that capability lightly. I do my job to the utmost of my abilities, and if that means playing your boss, I'll do it. You play your role, and we'll be just fine."

Custer motioned at the open airlock, which had a dusky gray view beyond. It was midday, but clouds covered the sky, some dark, others menacing. It wasn't a great day to be outdoors.

Rivka returned the gesture. "After you."

"Of course." Custer took one last look down the corridors of *Wyatt Earp* before stepping through the airlock and walking down the ramp. A ground car waited not far away. "Your people think of everything."

"We've been at this awhile, and they're SIs. They don't forget little details like scoring a ride for the boss."

Rivka walked to Custer's right, the traditional place of the higher-ranking individual. Custer stayed to the side and fell back half a step.

"The game is afoot, eh, Alberta?"

"I'll never forgive whoever came up with that name. May bedbugs infest the sheets of their life." She knew who it was. Clevarious. The SIs had scoured the web for an innocuous name that wouldn't trigger any of the suspected people they'd be dealing with. Alberta Finkelstein.

Anything new on our elusive Mr. Gamble? Rivka asked Clevarious.

Nothing. Your persona is now firmly established and back-

dated through an entire career. It would take a savvy SI to figure out what we've done, and I'd like to think those are all on our side. Also, Red is in the Pod-doc, completely voluntarily, although grudgingly.

Rivka chuckled.

"What?" Custer asked.

"Just thinking of my crew watching every move we make," Rivka lied. "I suspect you probably have a tracker embedded somewhere on your person."

"They wouldn't."

Rivka looked away. No, they wouldn't, but that didn't mean she couldn't take pleasure in his discomfort while he searched for a bug that wasn't there. She shrugged one shoulder.

"If Ash finds a bug, we'll both be dead."

"First time?" Rivka asked before they reached the waiting vehicle.

"Yes. Upon reconsideration, I should never have accepted Grainger's generous offer."

"By generous, I think you mean he threatened to pull your license if you didn't?" Rivka guessed.

"Something like that. The hook was working with you, which appears to have been a mistake on my part. You're married?"

"No. I just said that because it would have been poor form to just stab you in the eye, but Tyler and I might as well be. In that sense, it's true. I have my partner."

"To think I had a chance. Your crew is buff—"

Rivka cut him off before he could continue. They were too close to the vehicle for any candid conversations.

"Game time. Expect everything we do and say from here on out is being recorded and transmitted directly to the bad guys," she said in a hushed voice behind her hand.

"In you go, Alberta." Custer held the door.

"You first. I'll not have your weasel face leering at my ass."

Custer's mouth fell open. Rivka stabbed a finger at the passenger compartment. The lawyer climbed in, and Rivka followed. She settled herself and looked out the window. *Wyatt Earp* was nowhere to be seen. They had cloaked the ship the second Rivka was on the ground.

Rivka was adhering to the single most useful tool in a counselor's kit: say nothing. Silence couldn't be reviewed for slips of the tongue. Silence gave nothing away.

The vehicle wound its way through traffic into the city. Despite the driver's attempts to start a conversation, neither Rivka nor Custer engaged. He gave up and turned on music instead, letting it fill the uncomfortable void.

They continued through a nicer part of the city and into an area that had no chance of winning the neighborhood of the week award. Slums. Vagrants. Ne'er-do-wells. People meandering through the garbage piled along the sides of the streets noted the vehicle's passing as an opportunity to steal whatever might be inside. Those down on their luck continued on their way when the opportunity for an easy mark passed them by.

"Can you wait for us? We shouldn't be long at our meeting," Rivka asked.

The driver turned down the music. "I'm only going to stop long enough for you to get out. If you take too long exiting the vehicle, I'll leave anyway, and your bodies will be dumped as I drive away."

"You don't like credits?"

"I don't want to lose my cab and my life. No credits can pay for those. I'll come back for you, but if you're not waiting for me on the curb, ready to dive in, I won't even stop, and I won't be back."

"Our client will not be pleased. We're going to see—" Before Custer could finish, the driver jacked the music to the max and stuffed a finger in his ear. Rivka winced. Custer covered his ears.

The assault of syncopated rhythms was too much. Despite the uncongeniality they faced, being outside in Baron's Hold was preferable to being trapped in the rave going on inside.

As they slowed at the mid-rise apartment building, the driver turned the radio down. "I don't want to hear no names. I don't want to know anything. Get out fast. Send a note to Dispatch when you need me with an exact time of arrival. Be out here, and make sure you're alone."

"What if we're not alone, but the others with us are nothing more than dead bodies?" Rivka asked.

"Just don't get any blood on the seats." The driver accelerated, then jammed on the brakes and skidded to a stop. The side door popped open, and Rivka jumped out. Custer slid across and was stepping out when the driver accelerated away. The barrister spun in a circle and landed on the pavement, barely avoiding the cab's screeching tires.

"Get up. You're embarrassing me." Rivka snapped her fingers and headed for the door.

The homeless took note of the well-dressed arrivals and hurried toward them. Custer got to his knees, then to his feet. When he was upright, he bounced on one leg. The homeless, little more than zombies shuffling toward him, gave him the impetus to hurry after Rivka. He hopped and limped inside. The homeless people tried to pull the door open after him. He threw himself against the wall and cowered.

Rivka pressed her face to the plastiglass. "Fuck off." She reached for her neutron pulse weapon, but that was in her Magistrate's jacket. She was wearing a smart suit jacket and carrying no weapons.

One of the homeless people barreled into the door and pushed it open against Rivka's hold. She powered a fist through the opening and punched him in the face. He was thrown back into the small crowd. She forced the door closed.

Custer poked the elevator button.

"No." Rivka pointed at the stairs. She had her back against the door and was holding it closed, but the assault had stopped. The individual she had punched lay unmoving. The others stared through the plastiglass. Rivka yelled over her shoulder. "I said, fuck off!"

The zombielike mob started moving away from the door.

"You want to walk up twenty flights of stairs?" Custer held open the door to the recently arrived elevator.

"Of course not, but that's what we're going to do. I'm not getting trapped in that elevator. Control the situation, Barrister. Inside that thing in this environment? We have no control. Up the steps, Sally."

"You're mean," Custer grumbled. He limped toward the stairs. "I think my leg is broken."

"Fine. Take the elevator if you want. I'll attend the meeting by myself if you don't show up, and I'm not coming to look for you."

He tried two steps and came back down. "There's no way I can make it up twenty flights on this leg." He pulled up his trouser leg to show the swelling and discoloration that meant worse bruising would follow.

"You should have exited the vehicle at the speed requested by the cabbie. You make your own luck, Custer, and today, you haven't done that. You're going to suffer, and it's all your fault. No one here cares who you are, and they *most especially* aren't going to cater to you. This is the real world, something you have studiously avoided in your career."

Custer feigned outrage. "I've been here before and met with my client."

"You've been in this building before?" Rivka looked skeptical. She took the first step. The elevator started to buzz from being held open too long.

"Blue Heron Four. We met in a civilized section of the city."

"Then you haven't been *here*." She tipped her chin up the steps. "Meet you up top. I hope you make it since I'm not done tormenting you yet. I have parsecs to go before I sleep." Rivka vaulted up the stairs two at a time. Once she was out of Custer's sight, she accelerated. It felt good to run in natural gravity. She reveled in the workout, using the short respite from Custer to clear her mind and prepare her for the meeting with the mob lackey.

She reached the twentieth floor and stepped out into a straight hallway. At the end, a six-legged being waited. With her arrival, he uncrossed his arms and took a few steps in her direction. The elevator dinged, and Custer gimped out. He stared at Rivka in disbelief.

"Tikabow," the being at the end of the hallway growled. "Who's the sheila?"

CHAPTER FIVE

Wyatt Earp, Blue Heron Four, Landing Field Epsilon 17

"Rivka better appreciate this. Look at me!" Red fumed. He was thinner and shorter, his face a shade narrower. He didn't look like the man mountain he'd been two hours earlier. "I'm a total puss!"

"You're not whatever you think that means, but you better get out there if you want to catch up to the Magistrate." Lindy crossed her arms. She didn't think he looked much different. The change would be enough to fool any digital recognition systems and individuals Red had met before. His voice was the same, though. "You'll need to not sound like you, though."

"I can do the squeaky my-balls-are-getting-crushed voice." He tried to pitch his tone higher but failed miserably and ended in a violent coughing fit.

"Maybe speak with a lower voice. That's what little men with big-man complexes do, isn't it?" Lindy offered.

"How would I know?" Red asked slowly and deeply.

"That's better." She swooped in for a kiss. "Clevarious,

41

can you find a ride for Red to go wherever Rivka went and drop him off about a block away? What clothing is appropriate for that location?"

"Oh, my," the SI replied. "To blend in, he would have to look like a vagrant. He can carry no tactical gear."

Red grumbled unintelligibly. "Tell Tyler to get me Reaper, Rivka's neutron pulse weapon. I'm not going into the perp's den unarmed."

"I wouldn't either," Lindy agreed. She left the cargo bay while Red jumped around, trying to orient himself to his new, smaller body.

Red tried lifting the big railgun, which was meant to be carried by someone in a powered combat suit. It was the same weight it had been. He test-lifted other objects, then ran for the airlock. He bolted past Lindy, who was standing in Rivka's doorway while Tyler searched the room for Reaper.

"Where are you going?"

"Gym."

"Door won't open." Lindy watched as it opened before he arrived. "I'll be damned."

"I need to test something." He disappeared inside.

"Did you check her jacket? It's always in her jacket."

"Hang on," Tyler mumbled from inside. Moments later, he emerged wearing a sheepish smile and presented Reaper to the bodyguard.

"Much obliged." She took one step toward the gym, and Red strolled into the corridor, chest puffed out and back ramrod straight.

"I didn't lose any strength," he stated proudly.

Lindy shoved Reaper at him, smacking it heavily into

his chest. He bounced back a step. "I told you you didn't need to be that big. How about you stay a more reasonable size, which is still bigger than anyone else on the crew?"

Red scowled. "I need to intimidate Rivka's enemies and anyone who might wish to do her harm. To protect, we create an impenetrable barrier between the bad and the good."

"We can do that without you blocking out the sun. We'll need to get the Pod-doc to change your face back, though. I don't like this one."

Red continued to scowl. "But this is my face." He slashed his most winning smile.

Cole and the three *amigos* strode down the corridor. They stopped, taken aback by the change in Red's appearance. The bodyguard was now barely two finger-breadths taller than Cole.

"What happened to you? I feel like I should kick sand in your face next time we're on the beach."

Lindy chuckled to herself and turned away so Red couldn't see.

"You and I are going to have words, but after I get back. If I want any lip from you, I'll peel it off my zipper."

Lindy punched him in the arm.

"Sorry. Got to go save the universe."

Cole held his hands up, wondering about the incomplete explanation. Red didn't share any more, though. They ran down the corridor toward their quarters, to which Clevarious had delivered the proper clothing. Red dressed in what was little more than rags.

"At least it doesn't smell." He checked himself out and looked at Lindy. "What do you think?"

"I'm married to a proper vagrant. Go me." She took a bottle from the small shelf inset next to the bed and sprayed Red with it. "Oh, crap!"

"*What the fucking hell?*" Red's nose curled at the assault on his senses.

"I probably should have done that in the corridor."

"No shit. What is that?"

"The stench you didn't have," Lindy explained. "Clevarious thought of everything."

Red wrinkled his nose and fled their quarters. In the corridor, he hid Reaper in an inside pocket that seemed to have been sewn in for just that purpose.

The hatch to Engineering opened. It was also the hatch leading to the Embassy of the Singularity. Ankh stepped through, along with Chrysanthemum, his spouse. The two strolled toward him, hand in hand. Red would have stepped aside for them to pass, but it was clear that they were coming to see him. Lindy leaned into the doorway of the quarters she shared with Red, keeping the door open to help air it out.

"Hey, little buddy," Red said in his friendliest voice. He always worried when Ankh showed up unbidden.

"Here," the Crenellian said. He held out a coin that looked to be made of platinum. Red opened his hand and reached out. Before Ankh dropped the coin into it, Chrys caught his arm and injected something into his wrist. He recoiled, but it was too late. The deed was done.

"What the fuck did you do?" Red rubbed the swollen red mark on his wrist.

Chrys peered at it. "Much more violent reaction than we predicted. Should we put ice on it?"

"I think ice, yes," Erasmus said, using Ankh's mouth. Erasmus was the sentient intelligence who shared the Crenellian's body. He produced a small spray bottle and spritzed a little on the injured spot. Red let them.

Lindy watched in fascination.

"I still want to know what you did to me, you toad-faced asswipe."

Ankh gave Red his emotionless look, complete with unblinking eyes. After a short standoff, he answered, "It's a low-power beacon, but one that the mob can't track. No one can track it but us. You can thank us later."

"I can thank you now, but I won't. How about we ask permission before putting things in Red's body?"

Ankh gestured at Red's new look, and Erasmus spoke again. "With everything else going on there, the tracker in your wrist is the least of your issues. It's the one good thing you have going for you."

"If you weren't two ambassadors wrapped in one little cheesedick package, I'd punch you right in the face. Left-handed because I'm merciful."

"Did you hear that, my love?" Erasmus cooed. "Red the Merciful."

"I think it's best if Red hurries up," Clevarious interjected, using the overhead speakers.

"On the road, Mister Stinky McSloppypants." Lindy shooed him toward the airlock.

Red couldn't think of a worthy rebuttal, so he did the next best thing. He flashed the middle finger and held it in front of Ankh's face. Then he pushed it in front of Chrys' face and ended with Ankh. "That one's for Erasmus. I didn't want you to feel left out, Mister Ambassador."

"I most assuredly did not feel left out. Thank you, Mister Stinky. Or should we call you Sprout?"

"Sprout? I'm bigger than you!"

"We can hardly see you. You're almost microscopic," Erasmus parried.

"So small," Chrys added.

"That's it. I'm going back in the Pod-doc."

Lindy caught Red by the arm. "You'll do no such thing. Rivka is out there with a real cheesedick, trying to infiltrate the mob. Stop fucking around and go do your job." She pointed at Red's face, then at Ankh, and finally at Chrys. "All of you."

"Jeez." Red ducked in for a kiss. Lindy held her nose. Red looked at Ankh and Chrys. "This isn't over."

"It'll be over when we rescue your dumb ass from imminent death and you find yourself on your knees, thanking us profusely."

"Stand by. We're almost there," Clevarious announced. "Roof delivery in ten seconds."

Red moved into the airlock and waited. The ship's SI opened the hatch, and he jumped the two meters to hit the roof running. The hatch buttoned up, and the invisible ship accelerated away.

Lindy stared at the empty airlock. Ankh stood beside her.

"It's never easy," she said.

"No. It is not," Erasmus agreed. The three returned to Engineering, where Ankh kept his laboratory, and secured the hatch behind them. Lindy remained in the corridor.

She perked up and smiled when she heard Dery coming.

He stood on Floyd's back while the wombat jogged down the corridor. He beat his wings to keep his balance. Lindy caught him and pulled him into a hug. Floyd kept running. The engineering hatch opened, and she jumped through.

He is a great man, Dery said.

"I agree. So are you, little man. He swears too much. Maybe we can work on him together after he comes home to us."

After his trial by fire.

Dery hopped into the air and hovered in front of his mother's face.

She wondered what he meant, as always, but there was no sense in asking him. "Your dad has passed every test he's ever been put through. He'll pass this one."

A tear escaped Dery's eye and streamed down his cheek.

Lindy froze. Her shoulders sagged, and her eyes fell. She cried until she slumped to the deck, then she leaned against the bulkhead and held her face in her hands. The ugly crying had taken her over. Floyd came back and forced her way into Lindy's lap. Dery settled next to her without any explanation. She hugged them both.

Red ran to the rooftop access and pulled on the door. It was locked. It opened out so he couldn't kick it in, but he could bend it. He kicked it hard in the middle, and the aging metal dented. One more kick and the door sagged inward. He pulled hard against the lock that was no longer tight in the frame. The mechanism came apart and fell onto the roof.

He wedged the door open and hurried inside. *Where's Rivka?* Red asked.

Twenty-first floor. I'm going to disable your chip to remove any signature the mob could use to track you. A second later, Clevarious was gone, and Red couldn't "feel" the chip inside his head. He looked at the lump on his arm, but the lump was also gone. Ankh's ice spray worked quickly.

"I'll be damned, little buddy. That could come in handy, but next time, let's not make it for self-inflicted wounds," Red mumbled as he headed down the stairs. He had fifteen stories to go to get to where Rivka was. He shuffled and stumbled down the stairs to practice looking like he wasn't a threat. On the correct floor, the numbers weren't there, but he knew which one it was because the one above had Twenty-two painted on the door.

He opened the door, tumbled through, and lay on the floor as if he were half-conscious. The hallway was empty. He got to his feet and looked one way, then the other. He took one step before he heard a door opening at the end of the corridor behind him.

"Fuck off," a gravelly voice called.

Red waved over his head, then turned and stumbled back to the stairway door.

The voice belonged to a six-legged alien, the likes of which he'd never seen. Red figured he could take him in a straight-up fight. The legs would be a hindrance except on a charge.

Red paused at the door, and the alien came running.

The bodyguard backed through the door and control-rolled down the stairs.

The alien, whose head was atop a tall neck connected to a horse-like torso, stared at Red, who lay in a crumbled heap on the next landing down. "Don't come up here again if you know what's good for you. Go stand in the acid rain. It'll clean off some of your filth."

Red grunted and pushed up, then fell back down. The door closed behind the alien.

Security for the meeting? Security for the one they're meeting? Red thought about how much he didn't know. He'd come into this blind, and now he'd have to figure out how to get close without letting Rivka see him. Closed-door meetings did nothing for his ability to protect her, and without his chip, he couldn't contact her.

You need to use everything you've learned in working with her for the last few years, Red told himself. *She's in there. Wait here for her to finish, and listen for any commotion.*

Red stalked up the stairs to stand outside the door. He looked into the dark corners of the stairwell to confirm there were no cameras watching, then pressed his ear to the door and listened intently, digging deep into the extra abilities his enhancements gave him. He zeroed in until he could hear the six-legged creature shuffling his feet. Red pulled up his collar to hide his face, sat down, and waited with his head leaning against the door.

CHAPTER SIX

<u>Twenty-First Floor, Mid-Rise Tower, Baron's Hold, Blue Heron Four</u>

Custer limped in front of Rivka and offered his hand. When the only other individual in the room didn't take it, Custer moved closer and thrust his hand out. The two men shook hands.

"This is Barrister Alberta Finkelstein. She's my new boss, and she wants in."

"Simple as that, huh?" The other man crossed his arms and glared at Rivka. "Take your clothes off, and let's see what you're made of."

Rivka yanked Custer around to face her and slapped his face hard enough to shake his brain. His eyes crossed, and he staggered. She pushed him away. "That's what I'm made of, and I'll keep my clothes on, thank you very much. This suit is most stylish, don't you think?"

Ash turned his frown into a reluctant smile. "I'm Asheka Burako. I think we might be able to do business. You know what we do, so we'll skip the preliminaries.

What we need this pudknocker for is top cover. Our people tend to get arrested with an annoying frequency. They can do a week or two in the clink but no longer than that. I need assurances. My colleagues and I have our businesses to run."

As much as Rivka wanted to look around the space and get insight into the one calling himself Asheka Burako, she didn't dare. Her discipline kept her eyes glued to his face. She risked a glance at Custer. He was moaning and rubbing the side of his face. She'd left the outline of her hand on it.

"Man up. A woman slapped you, and you're crying like a baby. If you curl up in the fetal position, I'll have Hex toss you out the window. The mobs below will pillage your body before you stop falling. Another ten more minutes, and you won't be recognizable—if you had any features left after a seventy-meter drop."

"You hit me." He looked at Rivka and turned to Ash. "You threaten to murder me. Haven't I done enough to earn a little respect?"

"I think that answer is clear. My deputy is doing eighteen months in Jhiordaan. He'll be useless when he gets out because Parole will be all over him. You need to keep my people out of prison. Do you understand?"

"I understand just fine, but if your people are going to break the law in full view of a high-resolution camera followed by taunting the camera, they shouldn't expect a lot of mercy. It was a huge win to keep it from being life. You should be thanking me." Custer slowly massaged his face. He bounced on one leg, then leaned against the back of the couch.

"No." Ash kept it short and sweet. "Would you have done better?"

"Of course. I'm better than him." She jerked her thumb at the barrister. "That's why I'm his boss."

Ash smiled while looking down his nose at Custer. "Maybe we've been dealing with the wrong lawyer this whole time."

"He'll assist me with the mundane legal work. Don't get me wrong, when it comes to courtroom tactics and making everyone feel like they're a part of the team, that's my department. Both of us will take care of business, and you take care of us."

Rivka held out her hand. Ash took it without playing further games. Her handshake was firm. Ash was not stronger than her, and his brief squeeze was met with equal resistance. His thoughts about her had nothing to do with the legal side. He wanted to dominate everything, so he saw her as a challenge. His goal was to bed her.

She had bad news for him, but that could wait.

Ash looked at her out of the corner of his eye while sizing up his previous lawyer.

"We could dispense with him in entirety. That would save us money."

Rivka hemmed and hawed and dropped the corners of her mouth while contemplating Ash's proposal. She finally made up her mind. "I don't think so. Money isn't the problem. It's getting your people out of the legal bind, especially if they provide the prosecutor with an overwhelming amount of evidence. Maybe it's easier to hire smarter people."

Ash turned his back on his guests and looked out the

window. "That is always our goal, but this business has its challenges."

Rivka itched to ask him what his business was. She wanted an on-the-record clarification from one of the mini-bosses. She wanted to ask him about Gamble, but both subjects were taboo. She was undercover. Her handshake with him had not revealed anything worthwhile. It had been too quick.

The thought of touching him again revolted her. She had many other cards to play.

Ash continued, "We have a plan to distract the Magistrates and their ilk."

Rivka was glad he wasn't looking at her since the best she could do was freeze instead of seeming confused or indifferent.

"Magistrates? Aren't those the bastards who operate outside the law? You're right in not wanting them in our business."

"*Our* business?" He turned to her and glared. "*You* aren't in this business. You're only an employee whose risk consists of getting yourself killed if you cross us. I don't need partners. We have lots of those. I only need unswerving loyalty, for which the pay is more than you'll deserve."

"Leading by fear isn't the best way to get unswerving loyalty. You can threaten me, but my life was forfeit the second we boarded a slaver ship and put them out of business. I've been in law enforcement, and my complaint was about the lawyers not putting people away. So I became a lawyer. I learned that the system is rigged. If you can't beat 'em… You know the rest of it. You don't have to threaten me, Ash. You'll find that I bite back because I don't care anymore. I'm going to get mine, then buy a small moon out back of nowhere to populate with horse-men and their massive dongs to bring me fruity drinks."

He turned toward the window. "I feel like we can do business, maybe far more than something as simple as your office defending my errant people."

"I'm not satisfied working the minions."

He turned on her, eyes flaring with anger until he schooled his emotions. Then he leaned back and forced an uncomfortable laugh. He stopped the charade. "You'll deal with me until I deem otherwise. Now get out." He blinked when he spotted Custer. "You're still here?"

"I am part of this deal. Don't kick me to the curb, Ash. We've done a lot of work together."

"You don't have one-tenth the backbone of Alberta. There *is* good news, though." Ash stepped back.

"And that is?" Custer asked. Rivka would have counseled against his speaking further, but she couldn't shut him down in time.

"You can barely see the handprint on your face." Ash roared with amusement, and this time it was real.

Rivka cleared her throat to cover her mirth. She had to remind herself that she could only alienate Custer so much. These people would have him killed. As much as she disliked what he'd become and that he'd been in bed with the mob, she didn't want to see him get murdered.

She could use that as one more nail in their coffin. Possibly bump it up to a capital crime and execute the perps one by one until the mob was no more. In that sense, Custer's life would have a greater purpose.

Still, she wouldn't be able to live with herself. "We can poke fun at Tikabow all day long, but I don't want to see any harm come to him. No one wants a three-legged pet."

"I think some people do. Those with more empathy than sense. I hear you." He looked at Custer. "Don't do anything to get yourself killed, *Tikabow*." Ash spat the name as if it befouled the air.

Rivka tipped her head and turned toward the door.

"Tomorrow night, you'll have dinner with me."

"I will not. Not in this foul place." She waved dismissively and opened the door.

"It will be in a nice place downtown. I'll forward the information to Tikabow."

"I look forward to it," Custer replied.

"You're not invited," Ash stated.

"Then I'll not be there either. It's for both of us or none."

Ash furrowed his brow and chewed his lip. "People don't usually talk to me like that." Rivka shrugged her indifference. "I wouldn't accept it from a man." She stared at him unblinking. "But I find you titillating while also believing you are far more than eye candy. I'll invite you both. Downtown. Information to be provided. Don't think we'll talk about work unless I believe we're secure."

"I would like to hear more about how you intend to distract the Magistrates since if they're looking into you, I want no part of any of this. You know that they can execute people on the spot?"

Ash looked at Custer and scowled.

"It's true, but they have to convict you of a crime. What

crime have you committed, Ash? None. That's the message we deliver. Always."

Dammit, Custer! Rivka thought.

Ash held out his hand palm up. Rivka looked at it, wondering if she was supposed to daintily lay her hand in his to receive the kiss of supplication.

Fuck that.

"We'll be on our way." Rivka walked out before Asheka Burako could embarrass himself further. Rivka expected he would be searching for everything there was to know about one Alberta Finkelstein. She wanted to give him plenty of time to find and parse the information to make sure she was legitimate.

She hadn't expected the turn this interaction had taken, but she could leverage that without letting him get handsy. If he tried to touch her, she'd beat him to within a finger's breadth of his life. No undercover assignment was worth selling herself.

They'd get him and his peers. Who were the partners? She wanted to roll them up, but she would settle for him and his immediate contacts.

In the hallway, she brushed past the Atchimorian called Hex. His thoughts were violent. That one contact was enough to convict him of murder and send him to Jhiordaan.

"In due time," she told him cryptically. He sneered as much as his face would allow. Custer gave the being a wide berth, limping worse than when he arrived. Rivka turned to head down the stairs. Custer pressed the button for the elevator. "You aren't even willing to walk *down* the stairs?"

He pointed at his leg. "With this bad wheel? No. I'd like to stay off it completely. Maybe you could carry me?" He had lost his friendly tone, which brought a smile to Rivka's face. *Clevarious, send a cab for us. Five minutes, and we'll be on the curb.*

"So be it. Meet you at the bottom." She stepped through the door. A body shuffled down the stairs one landing away. "You there. Hold up."

A hand snaked out and gave her the finger.

Rivka laughed. "Or not." She hurried down the stairs, and the body huddled in the corner, back turned to her. She brushed him to get a quick look. Was he a foe?

She immediately realized who he was despite his thoughts of "Don't recognize me. I'm not him."

She slapped him on the shoulder. He cowered more.

Rivka continued before anyone could notice the brief exchange. She flew downward, jumping three stairs at a time, leaving Red far behind.

She reached the bottom and waited. Custer appeared a few seconds later.

He gimped out, and she moved close. "Put your arm over my shoulder."

He held onto her, uncomfortable about having to do so. Uncomfortable at having lost his status as the dominant member of the team. He was the least dominant of every involved party, and that included the wombat. At least she had the crew's love.

Custer teared up.

"It can't hurt that much." Rivka sounded skeptical.

"I can take the pain. It's all of it. I'm a big fucking nobody. You just proved that. Ash would just as easily kill me and move on. The credits in my account? Meaningless.

You've never had to deal with that. The realization is hard on someone like me, who's always been enamored of my own success. Finding it illusory is tearing apart my very soul."

Rivka glanced out the door. The taxi had not yet arrived. She pushed him into the wall. "Listen up. Your life is yours to live. How do you think I felt after murdering your client? I was going away for a crime *I* committed. I did it. I knew I did it. I didn't know why, but once it's over, you can't ever go back. You can only go forward and try to make things right. It was at that moment I realized I didn't like you. I didn't want to be like you. I even felt sorry for you.

"My life is different now. Light-years better. I have everything you thought you had, but I have it for real. That's the difference between us. That will always be the difference. Now, buck up and start living like an upstanding citizen. Stop being a weasel."

"Weasel." He chuckled. "I was thinking more along the lines of a sellout."

Thirty seconds, Magistrate, Clevarious said.

Rivka waited for fifteen, then helped Custer out the door. "Is the taxi coming? We'll be killed!"

"By the moons of Antares, will you get a grip? You just told me how miserable your life is, but you want to keep living it. The taxi will be here momentarily."

"How do you know?" He was looking at her instead of down the road, where the cab was maneuvering evasively to avoid derelicts and other vehicles that were driving just as recklessly.

The cab slid to a stop, and the door opened. She tossed

Custer in and threw herself after him. A second later, the tires squealed, and the car shot back onto the road.

Rivka lifted her head to look back at the doorway to see if Red had made it out after her. The space in front of the mid-rise was empty.

CHAPTER SEVEN

Wyatt Earp, Blue Heron Four, Landing Field Epsilon 17

Rivka stormed through the airlock. "I want everyone in the conference room right now!"

Custer tried to keep up but couldn't. He surrendered and stopped to lean against the wall. Before Rivka turned the corner at the entrance to the bridge, she looked back.

"Somebody get him into the Pod-doc and fix him!" she shouted at the overhead.

Clodagh waved from the captain's seat, but Rivka rushed past. Tiny Man Titan launched off Clodagh's lap, which he was sharing with Alanna. He yapped and bounced, stopping at the hatch to let Rivka's retreating form know about his dismay.

She stopped. He stopped. She turned. He ran.

Rivka continued to the conference room at a more subdued pace. Floyd bounced out of her quarters. "You called?" Tyler asked, holding the door to the stateroom open.

"You have a patient. Fix him, please."

Tyler wagged his finger at her. Her lip twitched in anger. "Santa won't bring you new toys if you keep breaking the ones you get."

"Santa?" Her snarl turned into a smile. "I'm surrounded by absolute lunatics." She raised her voice to a near-scream. "Everyone think about why Red was in that building with me. You're all in on it. I know it. You, too."

Not Floyd! a small voice cried.

She stared at Tyler. He strolled by, dipping in to kiss her cheek. She didn't stop him.

"Yes. We did it. We're not sorry. Red was going whether we were smart about it or not, so there you are. Are you going to spank me?"

Rivka relaxed. "Why can't I stay mad at you knuckleheads?"

"Because you love us, and we love you, too. No one will ever do anything to intentionally hurt you."

She grumbled, "I know." She loudly blew out her breath. "Maybe just this once, a plan can go according to…well, the plan."

Tyler howled as he continued down the corridor to find his patient. "That's a good one," he called over his shoulder.

Rivka crossed her arms and leaned against the doorway. Pounding feet signaled that the crew was running to join her. Everyone had been properly energized by her apparent mood. She couldn't stay angry with them, but she needed to lay things out clearly for the next steps.

Clodagh and the pilots were first. Next was the Bad Company squad. Already, there were going to be too many.

"Cargo bay." Rivka pointed.

Clodagh stayed in the corridor, a toddler in one arm and a dog in the other. "I'll tell the stragglers."

"Let Clevarious do it. He's still in the doghouse with me."

"What did I do?" the SI replied.

"You knew before this case started that you were going to Pod-doc Red and shrink him. That's why you blocked him out of the gym."

"You saw that, did you?"

Rivka did her best stunned-mullet face. "I think everyone in the universe saw that."

"Not all who wander are lost, Magistrate," Clevarious replied.

"Enlightenment will not be found down the path you're trying to lead me. I'm onto you, C. You might be the ringleader. When will you get a SCAMP body so we can toss you off the ship?"

Tyler appeared at the end of the corridor, helping a limping Custer. Chaz, Dennicron, and Chrys followed at Custer's gimpy pace since they couldn't get by.

"Magistrate, I feel attacked. I'm ready to swoon." Clevarious let his voice trail off and finished with the sound of a body hitting the deck.

"It's broken," Custer announced as if that vindicated him.

Rivka's patience instantly shot to zero. "You got out of the car too slowly, dumbass."

Tyler bit his tongue and hurried the lawyer into the cargo bay.

"We feel left out!" Chaz exclaimed. He harrumphed and jammed his hands on his hips.

"You?" Sahved asked from behind Rivka. "If this were a book, it would be the seventh chapter before anyone noticed I haven't been around. I'll have you know I've been studying to be a proper legal eagle, but I want to be included in the current case, too. We're one team!"

Rivka rubbed her temples.

"Why are you dressed like that, and where's your Magistrate's jacket?" Sahved wondered.

Rivka motioned for everyone to go into the cargo bay.

"No betting lines?" a voice bellowed from inside the cargo bay.

"Are you happy?" Custer snarked.

Rivka scowled while bumping past and through people to get through the airlock. She considered stepping on Custer's foot, but that was pettier than she was willing to go. She eased to the side to let them get through and to the Pod-doc, and Custer gingerly climbed inside.

After the lid was secured, Rivka leaned close to Tyler. "No augmentations. Just fix his leg. I don't want to have to deal with him having any kind of special abilities."

"I understand. One and done. Fix and fly. Bandage and boogie. Heal and hightail."

Rivka smiled at him. "The stress of what we do has changed us all."

"Made us lovably weird, is what you mean."

"I'll go with that." Rivka hopped up on a chair and waved her arms to get everyone's attention.

Chrys maneuvered Ankh to the front so he could see. It appeared to be against his wishes since she pushed, and he resisted. He had no hope of winning a battle of strength with a SCAMP.

"Ankh, Erasmus. My compliments to the ambassadors." She bowed her head. That calmed Ankh down. He looked up at her like the rest of the crew. "Atticus Tikabow is a lawyer who traditionally defends the worst criminals. He has a great record of winning those cases and freeing people who have no business being free. He's the reason I'm a Magistrate. He won a case, and the murderer walked free…until I caught up with him in a dark alley later.

"That got me condemned to Jhiordaan since I didn't deny it. I had done it. I committed the crime. I did the wrong thing for the right reason, but the High Chancellor could see that I had a gift. He challenged me to use that gift in support of the Federation.

"I can see into other people's minds. I know right away if they're guilty or not. I can see the crime. That's also a curse. No one should see anyone else's thoughts or feel their emotions, but here we are. For this case, I'm undercover with the goal of finding the head of the mob and decapitating it while taking out as many underlings as possible. We have one, the individual we met with today, but there are bigger fish out there. I think Tommy 'Silver Tongue' Gamble is a fake. I believe they're using it to distract us, so we'll need to string them along.

"You follow that lead while leaving us here, me and Atticus. I feel like Blue Heron Four is at the root of this more than our contact would have us believe. We'll continue to dig deeper until we find our next step. Yes, Atticus is a putz, but he's coming around. Maybe after we dismantle this organization, he'll stop defending certified scumbags."

"Ma'am." Furny raised his hand. "Two things. We stand

ready to go whatever the task." He nodded to his fellow warriors, and they nodded back. "Second, there doesn't seem to be any betting lines on this case."

Rivka clenched her jaw.

The flutter of wings in the silence signaled that not everyone had been in the cargo bay. Lindy entered with Dery. She looked like a wreck.

Rivka vaulted off the chair, tipping it over in her wake, and rushed to her bodyguard. "What's wrong?"

She snuffled before speaking. "Dery saw something bad happen to Red."

Rivka froze. "Then we get him out of there. Contact him and let him know we're on our way."

"His comm chip is off, so he doesn't radiate a signal, but Ankh inserted a different tracker in his arm."

"I used my comm chip in that building. What do you know that I don't know?"

"Nothing, Magistrate!" Clevarious replied. "We thought it a prudent safety precaution. We have no information to suggest there's much technology of any kind in the mid-rise where you met Mister Burako."

Rivka ushered Lindy to a chair and had her sit down. Dery hovered nearby. "What did you see, little man? You'll have to be specific."

Dery flew close so he could touch Rivka's cheek, but he didn't say anything.

"Not even a little philosophy?"

The river polishes the stone not by violence but by perseverance.

Rivka closed her eyes for some moments, then shook her head. "I got nothing."

Lindy hunched over, resting her elbows on her knees to hold her head up. Dery landed on her shoulder and folded his wings back. He stood looking up at Rivka, then seemed to notice the crowd. He waved at them with the hand of a five-year-old boy while carrying the wisdom of the faerie race.

The Magistrate returned to the chair, straightened it, and stood on it again.

"I need you to do nothing to help me until I ask for it. I can't be surprised by seeing Red lurking in the corridor outside our meeting with the mob boss. If he gets caught, our lives are in jeopardy. We can't go in there with warriors in power suits since we're looking for information.

"I need more from Burako without letting him know who I am. He needs to volunteer the information so we can roll up the whole organization in one pop. That's our goal. If he's onto us, then the perps will disappear like cockroaches when you turn on the light."

"We dropped him on the roof. I ordered that," Clodagh admitted.

Rivka waved her hand dismissively while staring at Ankh. "You chipped him. Now tell us where he is so we can go get him."

Ankh stared back, not blinking for an inordinate amount of time.

Chrys finally answered for him. "We can't see it this far away. Its range is far more limited than we anticipated. We have to be within two hundred meters of him, but we are making revisions to the chip now to extend the range."

"When will that be ready?" Rivka asked, rolling her finger to show her sense of urgency.

"We're modifying a future chip. The firmware is already in Red's wrist. We can't modify that version as long as it's there and not here." Chrys pointed at the deck.

Rivka nodded since she couldn't trust herself to speak. "Turn on his comm chip."

"It's not coming back on. We'll need to manually reset it," Chrys replied, once again pointing at the deck.

Red had to get back to the ship to fix all the things that would help him get back to the ship.

Ankh furrowed his brow. "Mistakes were made. We are looking to rectify them, which we can only do from my lab."

Rivka nodded once and pointed with her head at the airlock that led to the interior of the ship. "The rest of you. You'll need to put on a convincing show that Magistrate Rivka Anoa is coming for crime boss Tommy Gamble.

"Sahved, you said I hadn't noticed your absence. You've been knee-deep in your legal studies, so turn those into legal speak and deploy it like drones on a search-and-destroy mission. Lindy, buck up. I'll find Red, and I'll bring him home.

"Warriors! Have your suits ready. When we take these guys down, and I say when, not if, they're going to fight back. I'll need you to show them the errors of their ways. Chaz and Dennicron, you'll be fighting the cyber battle. They'll be searching for Alberta Finkelstein while we show them we're looking for Tommy Gamble. Convince them Alberta exists. Chase Gamble until I catch the ringleaders.

"Clodagh, Aurora, Kennedy, and Ryleigh, fly like the

solar winds. Make *Wyatt Earp* sing. As soon as Custer is able to walk, we're hitting the ground. We'll stay in the city, and you get out of here. Chase the ghost."

Rivka jumped down and joined Tyler at the Pod-doc's control panel. Tyler told her, "He'll be fixed up momentarily."

CHAPTER EIGHT

**<u>Big Bopper Bistro, a Hotel in Blue Heron, the Main City
on Blue Heron Four</u>**

Rivka looked at the desk clerk. Nothing changed. "There's only one room," she reiterated.

"Of course, we're happy to take it," Custer said with a big smile.

"With one bed." It was getting worse with each passing second. "You can take the couch."

"There's no couch."

"Send up three extra pillows and a blanket, please, for my esteemed colleague. I assume there's a floor." Rivka raised her eyebrows. The clerk nodded. "I thank you. Your credit chip?"

The woman fished in her pocket and held it out. Rivka tapped for a fifty-credit tip. "I don't know what to say. We still only have one room."

"But you do have extra pillows and blankets?"

"We do."

"Then we'll be fine." Rivka smiled at Custer. He winked at her.

Rivka's hand started to come up of its own accord. She caught herself before she backhanded him into next week.

Why do you use violence to solve your problems? he had asked. She hung her head. She was used to dealing with the worst of the worst when they left her with only one choice. That wasn't an unfounded threat, but overwhelming violence delivered harshly and instantly. What would it take for her to turn that off?

She wasn't sure she wanted to. They took their keys and headed for the lift.

"You're not going to run up the stairs?" Custer asked.

"I know what you're doing, especially since your broken leg is fixed and you're feeling all feisty. You're trying to push my buttons, and I don't understand your logic in doing that. I slapped you in the head to earn credibility with our contact because that's how you deserve to be treated. All he wants is to sleep with me.

"It seems that's what you want too. I'm not amused by either of you. If you magically appear in my bed, I will break both your legs before tossing you out the window. You'll splatter on the pavement below. We will not attempt to bring you back from that. You'll be scooped up with a shovel, and I'll rule it a suicide.

"Are we clear? You need to stop your bullshit, or I'll do this solo."

"I don't want to sleep with you. You're mean," Custer said barely above a whisper.

Rivka snorted. "Thank you. At least I ordered pillows

for you. Otherwise, you'd just be on the floor. I think that makes me kind, not mean."

"Mean as a snake," Custer reiterated.

Rivka decided she was done with the verbal jousting. She had real issues on her plate, like being alone while trying to find Red without *Wyatt Earp* and her crew to back her up. She wondered if anyone else had hopped off the ship to provide support. She hoped not.

But as Terry Henry Walton always said, hope was a lousy plan. She knew deep within that she had more than herself and Red to worry about.

Baron's Hold, Blue Heron Four

Red teetered and tottered as he walked slowly around the building. It had been hours since Rivka left. He didn't think she would come back until the next day, so his plan was to follow Asheka Burako and learn more about the mini-boss. If there was a threat to Rivka, it would come from him or his minion, the ugly-ass six-legged centaur.

"Mine! Go away," a gruff voice called from under a pile of garbage.

"Down on my luck, buddy. I was hoping for a scrap to eat. Don't take it personal."

"Personal! You're all up in my business. How could I take it any other way? You're a proper scallywag, you are."

"I'm pretty sure I'm not." Red tried to peer through the garbage to see who he was talking to. "Do you know anything about the people who live here?" He jerked a thumb over his shoulder.

"Them's the questions get ones killed in these parts."

"I have a few credits. Not many, though. Like I said, I'm down on my luck. I want to know who to avoid as well as who might be kind to people like us."

"You're not like me, and why would I want to give up my mark?" The voice sounded less angry. Red felt like he was getting to him.

"Because credits. If you don't, I'll give you the finger, tell you to fuck off, and be on my way."

"Then you better get to it. Come on now, asswipe. Give me the finger."

Red appreciated the bum's confrontational attitude. Red sat down instead. "Nah. You seem like a good egg. Here." He tossed the guy a chip with twenty credits on it. He had a small stash in his pocket that Clevarious had put in there for an occasion just like this. C was well ahead of all of them.

A skeletal and dirty hand snatched the chip out of the air and pulled it into the darkness. "Twenty credits! I ain't seen a twenty in many a year."

"How do you live?" Red asked.

"Barely," the voice replied. "Unlike you. I feel like you're not really down on your luck." The voice had changed from uneducated to more executive.

"It's a start. I've nowhere to go. The old lady threw me out. She was the one with the fortune. Better than I deserved. She finally decided that, too, and tossed me out with nothing but the clothes on my back and a few credit chips. It wasn't enough to get a place, so I'm trying to find my way. This is a hard world. I'm too old to be scraping dumpsters for a few calories to keep me going."

"*You're* too old? You look to be about twenty. Try doing this when you're fifty."

Red shook his head. "I'd rather not. So, what do you know about the people inside? I went up to the twenty-first floor and was met by a rather uncongenial six-legged fucker. He looked like he wanted to kill me. I got the hell out of there. Who was he protecting, and how does he leave? I want to make sure I'm nowhere near there."

The old man thought long and hard before answering. "Underground garage. Right over there."

Red had to assume he pointed. He couldn't see the individual. Behind the building was a depression, and behind that was a rusty gate. It looked like a utility access.

The voice lowered until Red could barely hear it. "His name is Asheka Burako, the one the six-legged creature works for."

Red hesitated. "How do you know that? Why would they ever tell *you* their name?"

"He didn't tell me his name. I gave it to him when he was born. I'm Antony Burako. He's my son. The six-legged creature is an Atchimorian they call Hex."

"Then why do you live out here?" Red wondered.

The individual finally crawled out from under the garbage. The smell that came with him made Red cough and cover his face.

"Because I made the man Ash became angry. This is where I live. I can go no further because he has deemed it so. Twenty credits." He handed the chip back to Red. "There are no stores within my perimeter, but I'd be obliged for twenty credits' worth of food if you would be so kind."

Red nodded. "I can do that. I'd like to hear more about that six-legged bastard. I feel like it's my destiny to fight him, and I don't fight to fight. I fight to win."

"You look like a fighter," the old man observed. He was missing a front tooth. He'd been on the wrong end of a punch in the mouth. He didn't miss anything, though. His eyes were clear and stayed in constant motion.

Red snorted. "I'm a shadow of my former self. You can trust me on that. I feel small and insignificant."

A rumble sounded from the underground access. "*HIDE!*" Antony yelled. He waved Red into his refuse pile. Old Man Burako stood.

Red moved until he had a view. He felt like he was lying in a cesspool. Maybe he was, but he'd struck gold. He wouldn't need to chase Burako. He'd learn what he could from the old man without seeming like he was trying to learn. Rivka would be pleased if he could bring something of substance to her—if he could figure out how to contact her without having his comm chip active.

A limousine rolled out. Red could see it through a small crack. It was small as far as limousines went. The six-legged being ran ahead of the vehicle to make sure the way was clear. The old man squared his shoulders and glared at the smoked windows.

The limo drove past, and the Atchimorian returned to the underground garage. The door rumbled closed. Red crawled out. Old Man Burako laughed at the look on his face. "You'll get used to it."

"I don't want to get used to it. Let me get you something to eat, old man, and then we can plot my revenge on that six-legged shitstain."

Chaz strolled through the high-end shopping district, nodding and smiling. People gave him a wide berth, so he revised his programming and approach to not make eye contact.

Then he blended into the crowd. *Do less, not more,* he counseled himself. Although he looked at the floor, his visual receptors picked up everything as if he were looking straight ahead. He also radiated a low-level millimeter-wave radar to pick up far more than what he could see or hear.

He linked through a nearby communications unit, riding a hidden message on the main broadcast signal. If an enterprising tech engineer tried to break it out, it would just sound like white noise.

He was looking for information regarding a reservation for three made for Asheka Burako. The Singularity was providing assistance since the planet of Blue Heron Four had no SIs. There were two EIs, Enhanced Intelligences, but they were of questionable loyalty and hadn't been contacted.

The Singularity would take care of it and relay the information when they had it. Until then, Chaz would mill about smartly, keeping the channel open. The hotel in which Rivka and Custer were staying was only a block away. Chaz used a low-level signal to ping her comm chip to let him know if she got too close. She wouldn't know he was doing it. He counted on humans not being as sensitive to their technology as an SI.

He was also monitoring Red's broadcast, which was an

extremely low frequency that didn't broadcast well through fluid, which made the chip's placement close to the skin critical. The insertion had gone deeper than desired, and Red's body had fought it by creating a pus sack around it, further limiting its effectiveness. The two-hundred-meter range was down to one hundred meters. Almost useless.

SIs didn't make mistakes like that. Chaz and the others continued their roundtables to figure out how they could have missed critical parameters like broadcasting ELF through a fluid. It was simple, and the SIs were kicking themselves.

Ankh and Erasmus had gotten into a huge argument over it, and the Crenellian had blamed it on Chrysanthemum being a distraction. Now none of them were talking to each other. Ankh had stormed off, which was problematic since Erasmus was part of him. They stomped back and forth virtually, neither getting out of the other's sight. Dennicron was playing referee, trying to solve the problem in a way that would help them find Red.

That was the bottom line. If anything happened to Red because of the SIs' failure, there would be hell to pay. It could cost Erasmus his ambassador position. They were counting on Red's abilities to keep him safe despite Dery's ominous warning. They had more confidence in Red than they did in themselves at the moment.

That could have been the shot heard around the galaxy.

Chaz strolled to a street corner under an overhang where he could watch a string of taxis arriving at the hotel to pick up customers and take them away. For what reason? Chaz didn't care. His only concerns were Rivka and Red. Everything else would have to fall into place. If Rivka did her job and Red did his, neither would have to know Chaz had been there.

A backup to the backup. Rivka was important enough to all of them that they would so brazenly defy her orders. They justified it by believing she was out of sorts, thanks to Custer. Her mood had turned dark, and she'd been at odds with normalcy since he showed up.

Chaz would have preferred that he was entirely out of the picture.

It wasn't his choice, and Rivka told them it hadn't been hers, either.

Since the case was secret, they didn't even have the regular betting lines to follow. None of the norms applied. Chaz was an SI, able to adapt and grow, but he found that he liked routine. He preferred one way of addressing a case since there would always be plenty of unknowns that needed to be reacted to, but not this time. It bothered him when he knew it shouldn't.

As Chaz's emotions evolved, he found it was harder to grapple with them. Then he started to question whether he was the right SI to be on the ground supporting Rivka while the others flew off to make believe they were hot on the trail of the elusive Tommy Gamble.

The Singularity couldn't find where Burako had made reservations for dinner. Chaz would have to watch for Rivka to leave the hotel. Then he would follow her.

CHAPTER NINE

<u>Grainger's Frigate, in Orbit over Delegor</u>

Buster Crabbe sat in the captain's chair, arms crossed, unamused. "Beau, I'd like to think we can resolve this ourselves. We don't need the other Magistrates. If Tommy Gamble is here, we'll find him and take him into custody before the rats can scurry off the sinking ship. Easy breezy, double-squeezy, ass please-y."

Beau, the frigate's SI, replied, "I'm pretty sure that's not the saying. High Chancellor Grainger said to wait here for *Wyatt Earp*, so that's what we're doing. I work for him. You are only borrowing his ship, which leaves me in the ghastly position of having to pseudo-answer to you. Ghastly, I tell you."

"What happened to you, Beau? You used to be more down to Earth. A good working stiff, blue-collar like me."

"That was before Magistrate Grainger was elevated to the lofty heights of High Chancellor. I am somebody now."

"You were somebody before," Buster argued. "So be it. Can you connect me to Chief Mak Elb Bint, please?"

"Are you sure that's a good idea?" Beau asked. "We're on a secret mission to catch a mob boss who's not supposed to know we're here until we spring the trap. I think I won't connect you to anyone. Are you okay, Magistrate Crabbe? Maybe you should read the briefing on this case once more."

"Maybe I should read the briefing on this case," Buster countered. "I thought I'd already read it, but I don't remember any of what you're saying."

Buster brought up the case on the screen. He skimmed it, looking for what he remembered, and couldn't find any of it.

"Do you have a record of what I last opened?"

"Yes. It was the attachment to this file, background information on Asheka Burako."

"No wonder none of this sounded familiar, hence my confusion on why we were at Delegor. Do you think the Delegador is still mad at me?"

"I am, so he probably is, too," the SI replied.

"Why are you mad at me?"

"Why wouldn't I be?"

Buster was going to continue arguing, but he knew it would get him nowhere. Grainger's SI was a master at diversion and projection. He was probably too snarky for his own good. Buster was a visitor on the ship, and that left him with no say in the matter, especially not to Grainger. He'd hold his tongue and requisition his own ship. Buster jumped up and headed for the galley.

"I thought you were going to read the case notes?" Beau wondered.

"I will. With a nice chai latte in one hand and the desire to excel in the other, what more could I lust for?"

"I'm truly at a loss," Beau replied.

Philko, Buster's SI partner, chimed in privately, *I can't believe you didn't read the briefing. I could have summarized it for you.*

I assumed what it was, and you know what they say. When you assume, you make an ass of you and umption. I didn't think you were here. Thanks for stopping by.

Yes, exactly that, Philko agreed. *Make sure you keep me involved even though I'm only with you in spirit, linked from our ship through Grainger's frigate. Erasmus tells me I'm next up for a SCAMP body. It won't be long until I'm mobile and can join you if you keep using Grainger's ride.*

It has the Gate drive. We're limited on our little ship until we can get one installed. Can you work the Singularity to hook us up? Buster requested.

I'll see what I can do, my friend. In the meantime, please read the case. When the time is right, you'll get to talk with your friend Mak.

You get me, Philko. Can't wait until we walk in together and own a place. Toss perps out windows left and right. It'll be glorious! Okay, it won't be. I'd prefer to sneak into the server room late at night, find the evidence, and put the perp away at a decent hour without a scuffle. Damn you, Magistrate! You've foiled my dastardly plans.

Philko chuckled. *You are spending far too much time alone, my friend. You need to get yourself a partner.*

I'll take it under advisement. Buster dismissed his friend. He liked being alone, mostly, even though with Philko, he never was. He looked forward to heading to the planet's surface and meeting with their head of law enforcement. Once they had the information that *Wyatt Earp* carried, they'd go in all guns blazing.

But not to get pizza and beer. The mob would never know what hit them.

Big Bopper Bistro, a Hotel in Blue Heron, the Main City on Blue Heron Four

Rivka and Custer waited for the limousine. Or it could be a taxi. The note from Burako was not specific. It came across as if he were playing a game, but then again, he was. It was the game of staying out of the limelight. He *was* a criminal, and he was proving to have a certain savvy that would make him difficult to pin down.

Until Rivka questioned him while looking into his mind. It would take less than a minute to convict him when she was able to do it her way, but he wasn't the one she had her eye on. It was the next one up in the chain and the one above him until the top levels were taken down. Without that coordination of the illegal drug supply chain, the entire system would collapse.

That was the real goal. Asheka Burako was simply a vehicle to get her closer to it.

So she could close the case and return to her people to doing her usual Magistrate work. "I really gotta get some time off. This is the fourth or fifth case in a row without a break."

"People tend to find the right level of stress for themselves. They will inevitably complain about it, but they do it anyway. To the edge of breaking because that's where they find the greatest satisfaction. That's where you are. I think your friction point is not getting the support of your crew for this case. I'm here for you. You're not alone."

"You were making great points until you dropped that last bullshit, and that's what it is. You are a liability. When shit goes down, I'll have to protect you instead of going on the offensive. If you get yourself killed, it will reflect poorly on my stellar record of not getting co-workers killed."

Custer snorted and lowered his voice. "It's probably because they're all enhanced by your Pod-doc."

"That's just another layer of body armor. We all work out like fanatics. When's the last time you hit the gym? You're looking soft, Custer. Maybe your name should be 'Custard.'"

"I'll have you know that I own the latest Pellytone strider and toner."

"That's nice. Do you actually use it, or is it just another trophy in your overpriced penthouse?"

"Such hurtful words! I use it. I didn't climb twenty flights of stairs because of a broken leg, and you think I'm a lightweight."

"You were a lightweight before you broke your leg," Rivka countered. She nodded at a limo that pulled up in front of them. Someone was in the back. The window descended, and Ash spoke through the opening. "Climb in. We're off for the best in a near-meat experience."

Rivka waited at the window. "Is that an innuendo?" She clenched her fists. Ash beamed at the challenge.

"You haven't been on Blue Heron Four very long, so you don't know. This is a vegetarian-only planet. They do not harvest bistok and you can't get it here, no matter how much you want it. They may look the other way on a lot of things but not meat. It's a tragedy."

"I'm fine with substitutes for a short while, but then I need the real thing," Rivka replied.

"That's far better than any innuendo I would have attempted. My compliments, Alberta."

Custer failed to control his mirth. The fire rose in Rivka's neck. If she were sandwiched between Custer and Burako, she would be even more uncomfortable than she already was. When she climbed in, she took the seat opposite Burako and motioned that Custer was not welcome to sit next to her. She crossed her legs and looked out the window.

"One of my people has been taken into local custody. I'll need you to have him released by this evening," Ash said like he was discussing doing the dishes.

"What jurisdiction?" Rivka asked.

"Does it matter?" Ash countered.

"A lot." Rivka waited for a more definitive answer.

"It's not actually on this planet. It's on a little place on the edge of the galaxy called Delegor. Have you heard of it?"

Rivka choked back the bile that instantly rose in her throat, thinking about Delegor cuisine. "Have you heard of the blood trade?"

Burako shook his head.

"That was out of Delegor and the neighboring system of Foromme. It was extremely lucrative, but the Magistrates took them down maybe six months ago. I've been lying low since then, looking for a new opportunity. And look, here you are. Delegor needs something to distract them from the rigors of their daily routine, along with how disgusting their food is. They could use a little Advantageous."

Burako pursed his lips while contemplating Rivka. He didn't let his eyes wander around her body as was his usual practice, but he focused on her.

Maybe she had said too much, but this was part of the background. Long periods where there was no record of her. She could fill it with whatever information she deemed fit.

"You've clearly been there. Not many people have." He continued to look skeptical. "The fact that your client was busted does not give me a great deal of confidence in your abilities. Why did you lose him?"

"We lost the inside track to sales because he let those idiots from Foromme run the show. My client was on Delegor. Don't eat the food, and most importantly, do not go into a restaurant and order anything."

"The food waste law. That is important." He let his tongue drift over his lips. "I'm still not sure about you. You can guarantee I'll check your story. If you're lying, you will suffer greatly."

Rivka forced a yawn. "More threats from Mister Small Berries. Do you have any other plays in your book?"

"Touché, Alberta." He gave himself over to looking out the smoky windows at the darkening city. There wasn't much to see besides bright lights marking the latest opportunity for people to share their hard-earned credits.

The limo continued for another ten minutes before making a hard turn off the main drag to accelerate down a side road. Rivka wasn't amused. Most kidnappings started with going the wrong way. If she only knew where they were headed.

But no. The limo pulled up to an overhang that covered a rear entrance for a place called Bangers.

"Classy," Rivka said, climbing out last. Burako and Custer offered their hands, but she didn't take them. She didn't want to see their lurid thoughts. When the time was right, she'd touch Burako's arm and ask the hard questions. He had information she needed. It was the only reason she was there.

Although she was hungry.

The sign raised her ire. Delegor's Finest.

"What the hell is this?" she demanded.

"It's a joke to keep the riffraff away. Anyone who knows regards this as the best restaurant on Blue Heron Four. Difficult to get a table on the best of days, but I'm me and have a standing reservation to use as I need."

"Of course you do." A doorman appeared to open and hold the door. Rivka gestured for Burako to go first. "It's your reservation. We won't stab you in the back. At least, not before we've eaten."

Ash threw his head back and laughed. "I don't know what your game is, but it is delicious!" He strode inside like he was the king of the universe.

CHAPTER TEN

<u>Somewhere in Blue Heron</u>

"Did you lose them?" Chaz asked the taxi driver.

"We were too far back. I didn't see which way they went. Sorry. I thought you wanted a ride, not to act out your own police chase fantasy. Maybe you should get out of my cab." The driver brandished a small bat with a metal strap around the end. He snarled to add to his menace.

At the speed of AI thought and SCAMP action, Chaz grabbed the club and ripped it out of his hand. He dropped it on the floor of the back seat. "I thank you for your valiant efforts in heavy traffic. I shall depart your vehicle now." Chaz paid the debt on his way out of the cab, then closed the door softly and strolled onto the busy sidewalk. Two separate people waved vigorously to get the driver's attention.

Chaz found a quiet spot against a building. People of all races passed by. Most were in a hurry, walking with a sense of purpose that suggested the workday was done, but the evening's entertainment was yet to start.

He attempted a low-energy ping of the Magistrate's comm chip, not enough to alert her. The response was instantaneous. She was less than two meters behind him. He turned slowly to find her staring through the window at him. Custer swallowed hard. Chaz turned back to the sidewalk and joined the flow of traffic.

He documented his approach and what he considered his failure for a full review with Dennicron later. For now, he'd move across the street and try not to let her see him again.

Even though it was too late.

He had been busted while doing the opposite of what she had asked, and thanks to Custer's lack of self-control, the whole case might have been blown. Chaz moped as much as one whose body was mechanical and operated at a certain efficiency at all times could. He was crushed by his lack of awareness.

It had been much easier when all he had to do was fly the ship and be there to help Rivka answer questions. That had been child's play compared to fieldwork.

Chaz's respect for Rivka grew with the realization, but he feared her respect for him was gone. He crossed the street with a crowd and found a spot a long ways away but within range of his eyes to magnify the view of Rivka and her companions. Despite watching them, he couldn't concentrate. Remorse and recrimination consumed his compute power. He set his systems on autopilot to record everything for later review. He could no longer trust himself to do the job in real-time.

· · ·

Bangers Restaurant, Blue Heron

Custer kicked Rivka under the table. She wanted to punch him. She also wanted to reach through the window and drag Chaz inside to deliver a comeuppance on a titanic scale. Instead, she smiled easily and turned to Burako.

"Ash, how does someone who lives in a mid-rise amidst squalor afford a standing reservation at the hottest place in town, along with a limousine ride to get here? That suggests you're not one to put on airs in business, only at play."

He glanced at Custer and then out the window before returning his gaze to Rivka. He was all about posturing and talking about himself, but he was unsettled by Custer's reaction. "What is it?"

"That dude looked familiar, but we left him in prison on Festus Three. Shit, man. I think he might be after me."

"What?" Ash was taken aback by the revelation.

"I might be wrong. We got a dealer off by pointing fingers at someone else, and that someone else did hard time. It looked like him, but then again, he didn't seem to recognize me. It couldn't have been him. He's still in the big house. He has to be."

Custer nodded while looking out the window, trying to see where the individual had gone. He shrugged after a fruitless search. "I guess not."

Burako wasn't convinced. "You saw something."

"He looked familiar, but you two fonkers have got me jumping at shadows with all your doom and gloom, and you'll both kill me if I look at you sideways. Well, you know what? Fuck you!"

Rivka snorted. Burako couldn't contain himself either.

"That's pretty funny. I'm not sure I've ever been called a fonker before. Maybe we'll keep you around a little bit longer."

Rivka laughed so hard that tears welled in her eyes, and she started to cough. She drank her water and signaled to the server to bring more. They had a server to themselves, another sign of wealth and power.

She finished, and Burako beamed at her. The purity of Custer's quick thinking was now behind them. Back to the jousting contest with the man who would be king. She was convinced he was a mini-boss but angling to be more. He would need to go at the right time. And despite his confidence, he was *not* charming.

Rivka leaned back. They had promised not to talk about work, but she maneuvered the conversation toward it. "What do you like most about Delegor?"

"Delegor can suck my ass. I don't like anything about it except that it's a good market. I'd say more, but no business talk. Tell me, why don't you grow your hair longer?"

"Because I'm not a young girl, and short hair is easier to manage. Why do you keep yours short?"

He hummed for a moment while looking at the ceiling. "I guess for the same reason. It's easy, but it's also masculine. I'm not going for the rugged barbarian look. I need to appear more cultured. It's important in my business."

"Is everything you do defined by your business?" Rivka asked pointedly. Custer had long been forgotten. The two behemoths were jockeying on the field of verbal combat.

"Is yours do business also?"

Rivka stared at him, wondering if she had heard the disjointed wording incorrectly, but she hadn't. "Mine business isn't blue sky," she ventured, jockeying his nonsense with some of her own.

"A well-used desk are not always maybe," Ash replied.

Rivka contemplated her answer, but a crash from the kitchen yanked their attention away from each other. Their personal server eased toward the wall. Two men burst into the dining area. "Put your credit chips on the table quick, and no one gets hurt."

"Will my lawyers protect me?" Ash whispered, holding his hands up. He hadn't put anything on the table.

"In court, yes. Here? I'm not offering up my body for science." She fished in her pocket for the scrubbed credit chip. It didn't have much on it, and it was coded to her fingers. No one else would be able to use it. Custer dug into his pocket, but Rivka stopped him and put her chip on the table. It was enough to cover all three of them.

The criminals hurried from table to table. The one collecting the booty stopped at Burako's table. "There should be three chips. Fess up." He crooked his fingers.

"You expect me to have a chip?" Rivka wondered. "I never!"

"Rich bitches always have money. Give it to me?" He lunged across the table. Ash caught his arm, twisted it, and dragged the man over the table and into the window. He slammed into it face-first and slid down to the floor.

Rivka ducked and recovered his weapon, a homemade pistol. She was afraid to pull the trigger.

She crouched with the weapon. The second criminal, a two-legged Yollin, was at a loss. He roared and gestured with his pistol that they were to help his partner up.

Sirens wailed outside. The Yollin lost his nerve and

bolted. The person on the floor started to stir. Ash kicked him in the face, bouncing the back of his head off the window. He lay still after he hit the floor. Burako stepped back to give him room.

"I guess that's it for dinner. My wine was wasted."

The server looked at the door to the kitchen before returning to the table. He couldn't decide what to do.

"To go, please. Takeaway for us since we won't be eating here. Put it on my tab."

"Of course, Mister Burako." The server went to the kitchen, checking it before going inside.

"What are you going to do with that?" Ash pointed at the gun in Rivka's hand. She placed it on the table and wiped her prints off with her napkin.

"Shall we?" Rivka suggested, tipping her chin toward the kitchen door.

"Leaving the scene of a crime?" Ash asked.

"There's no competent authority here to instruct us otherwise, and I have zero desire to answer any questions. The restaurant staff can tell them all they need to know."

"I like the way you think."

Custer finally joined the conversation, rubbing his hands together to keep them from shaking. "Deny everything." He hurried in front of the other two and burst through the kitchen door, nearly mowing down their server. Everything had stopped while they were trying to process what had happened.

The server held his hands up. "Your food isn't ready."

"It's okay. Sometimes bad things happen to good people. Go make sure everyone gets their credit chips back." Ash pointed with his thumb and continued to the back door. The limo had turned around and was waiting.

Ash opened the door and peeked at the driver. "Those punks didn't cause you any problems, did they?"

"No. Why should they? They looked like staff. They used a key and walked in, then that Yollin came out of there in a hurry. First time I thought something was up. I'm happy to see you're okay, Mister Burako."

"We're just fine, Rudy. Take us through the Choke N' Puke drive-through. We'll grab something to go."

Custer climbed into the vehicle, continuing to rub his hands together. Rivka and Asheka looked at each other, then at Custer. "Man, you gotta toughen up," Ash called to him before climbing in. Rivka was last in and took a seat next to Custer since Ash sat on the opposite side. He dipped his head in recognition of her consistent desire not to sit next to him.

The limo accelerated down the alley.

Rivka wondered what Chaz was thinking about what had happened. She had learned nothing that evening except that Asheka Burako had some training and wasn't afraid of a punk with a homemade pistol. He was able to handle himself. He'd probably worked his way up from muscle to management.

There had to be some upward mobility in the mob. Maybe they had a university. Hard Knocks U? Rivka kept herself amused while giving the side-eye to Custer, who was deteriorating into a quivering mess. He'd handled spotting Chaz well, but the sight of the gun and getting robbed was more than he could handle.

"Maybe you can take us back to the hotel. I doubt this

one is good for anything. We'll order room service or something."

Ash nodded and called the new instructions to the driver. Once the driver acknowledged the return to the hotel, Ash focused his attention on Rivka. "Them are wasn't," he said, continuing the earlier game.

"Can't not know," Rivka replied. "Nothing you could have done. Nicest restaurant in town gets rolled. That's some serious bullshit right there."

Burako chuckled. "It is. I wanted to show you the best Blue Heron has to offer. Instead, I show you the absolute worst. The dregs of society live here. Maybe there's nowhere left for decent folks. Not here, anyway."

"How has addiction affected that?" Rivka asked pointedly.

"I've heard the military has a phrase. 'Don't crap where you eat.' There's more wisdom there than meets the eye. I should consider leaving. This planet can devolve into the cesspool it was destined to be."

It's your fault, Rivka thought. *We'll take care of that problem soon.* She smiled at Asheka Burako. He had no idea.

CHAPTER ELEVEN

<u>Baron's Hold, Blue Heron Four</u>

Red returned after three hours. The old man was alert, only his eyes visible in the darkness of his filthy cave. "What took you so long?"

"It seems that people don't believe you've got credits when you look and smell like this." He gestured at himself. "I had to pass a credit chip through a window before they got me anything, and I think they ripped me off."

"What's new?" The old man took the plate hungrily and started to eat using his fingers.

"I brought utensils and a napkin." Red offered them. The old man took them and tucked them away. He continued eating with his fingers.

"This is the nicest thing anyone has done for me in ages. What's your hook? Are you gay? You look gay. I'm not like that."

Red thought the old man was trying to get his goat. He brushed off the remarks. "With the smell in this place, I doubt anyone is feeling frisky. I can't imagine how. No, old man. I have a wife and son somewhere." Red didn't want to reveal any more.

"Ha!" Antony Burako didn't ask for more information. He didn't pry. He did what good vagrants did and minded his own business. That taught Red he needed to be more patient and settle in for a long evening. He'd catch up with Asheka Burako when he returned to work on the morrow.

"Mind if I squat here for the night?" Red asked.

"Stay outside. This is my place."

"Sure. I'll stay out here. You got nothing to worry about from me. I can't speak for these other shady characters skulking about. They strike me as needing a daily beat-down to keep them from acting the fool."

"You talk funny and too much." Antony belched and shuffled into the heavier darkness. Soon, everything grew quiet. Red listened intently and heard a slight wheeze, slow and rhythmic. The old man was asleep. He probably only snagged an hour here or there. Red had seen pack behavior while he was out. What had taken so long was giving them the slip so they didn't follow him back here.

Anyone who bought food was a target. Red expected them to show up and sniff around late that night. Nocturnal hunters would scuffle about in the darkness like the rats they were.

It made Red wonder who had money to buy drugs. Why was the drug trade so prevalent on a hellhole like Blue Heron Four?

Maybe it wasn't anymore. It had been, and that was why the planet had deteriorated. Now it was time to move on.

Many other planets were prosperous, like Delegor.

Prosperous enough. They'd been told the mob was using Delegor as a diversion.

Red was confused, but he knew one thing. If he was to get any sleep, he'd need to go on the offensive. He was tired and hungry.

He slipped into the shadows and stalked away from the cesspool Antony Burako called home. He peeked around the corner far enough to see if anything was coming, moving at a glacial pace. Quick movements could be seen, while slow movements were just another shadow, making the observer question whether they'd seen anything. Red froze against the wall and watched.

The gangs would come. He was sure they were coming for him, an easy mark who had money. They had seen past his disguise, or they didn't care. Anyone who had more than they did was rich.

Red, a rich man. That made him laugh, although he had everything he wanted. He would never take that lightly. Maybe he *was* rich.

A shadow flashed through another shadow, followed by more. The gang. He counted seven. They were denizens of the slums, barely more than skin and bones. They'd be vicious, but they were no match for Red in any number.

He waited as they flowed toward him, an inexorable tide of envy. He pressed into the shadow until he became one with the wall. The gang passed him, barely making more noise than the wind brushing the sidewalk. When they were by, Red hurried after them and caught the last one. He yanked him back and cut off his air until the young man passed out. It would have been easier to kill them, but that wasn't his charter. If they attacked him, he would make them wish they hadn't.

He deposited the unconscious gang member in a dark corner and followed the others, taking the place of the one they expected to see.

Red caught up to the sixth and punched him so hard in the back of the head that the youngster was out cold before he fell. Red showed his speed and dexterity by catching his victim before he hit the ground. And the next, and the next.

Only three left. They noticed something was wrong, and as one, they stopped and turned.

"You're in the wrong place, boys," Red said. "You can gather up your fellows and be on your way, or you can get your asses kicked, too."

Red thumbed the neutron pulse weapon to level one and activated it. He aimed it at the closest and panned to the farthest. The youngsters vibrated at the assault on their cells. They didn't know what was wrong, but they didn't run away like they should have.

"Fuck that guy!" one said, trying to sound brave. They were missing four of their gang, but there were still three of them. Courage in numbers.

Red needed to take them out before they adopted a strategy. He stalked toward them, coming out of the shadows so they could get a good look at him. They realized he was much bigger than them, but they were cornered, at least in their minds. Red gave them an escape, but they didn't take it. They only saw one way—straight through him.

The three punks came at him at the same time. Red dodged left hard and sprinted to the side to place the building at his back. Facing them, he crouched, feinted right, and swept his leg to the left, tripping the one in the middle. He dove to his right, blocked the shiv, and hammered a fist into that punk's face.

He caught him by his shirt and threw him into the youngster who was trying to get to his feet. Red kicked the youngster in the face like a punter sending a ball high into the sky. Two were out of action. Red headed for the third, who took off. One out of seven had the wherewithal to do the right thing.

Red left the scene at a run. When he was out of sight, he slowed and became one with the shadows. It was his intent to clear the two blocks in every direction. Then he'd return to Antony's cesspool and get some sleep. If the punks organized, he'd use the neutron pulse weapon to execute their leader. Then the rats would scatter. The lesson would be learned. *Don't come into this area. There is a new sheriff in town.*

The next gang was smaller but took the same amount of convincing. Three had to be knocked unconscious before the fourth fled. After that, the only ones roaming the street were those with nothing to fear because they had lost everything. Not even the punks' torment gave them pause.

To be afraid, you had to have something to lose.

Red told them to seek shelter outside the mid-rise tower. He was going on a food hunt. He had more credit chips that could be put to good use. Despite how tired he was, he hurried four blocks away to the only open store, which was protected like it stored gold bullion.

The clerk from earlier wanted him to pass a chip through the window again.

"How about, 'Fuck no?'" Red snarled. "You ripped me off last time. I'm coming inside to shop. You'll ring me up, and I'll pay the bill."

Red pulled his shirt sleeve up to show his well-muscled forearm, which was not the arm of a vagrant.

The clerk relented and let him in, locking the door after the bodyguard entered. Red looked at the prices and bought what he could get the most of for the least amount of credits. Protein and filler. He went a little more expensive to get stuff that was healthier. It took two of his pre-loaded credit chips to pay the bill. He took his armload, thanked the clerk, and headed into the night.

He stayed in the shadows and moved slowly to throw off anyone who was tailing him. He made a circuitous route back, collecting the homeless and downtrodden on his way.

When he reached the mid-rise, he would have started handing out the food, but the gang had found its backbone despite the bruises. The group of seven had become fifteen. Red couldn't put the groceries down. The first homeless soul would take them and run.

He could always buy more. He grabbed two of the people he'd sent to the mid-rise tower. "You will guard these with your lives. Do you understand me? I need to take care of these punks, and then we're going to do right by the rest of you." Vacant eyes returned his look. "Stay here."

He turned his attention to the group of young toughs.

"All of you. Send your toughest. Give him that bat. Let

him bring the pain. I'm here. I got nothing but my bare hands."

"We saw what you could do with your bare hands," one of them said.

"We have a spokesman. Come on out, tough guy. Let's see what you're made of. Or are you too weak to show your face? Afraid you might get a fist in it?"

"We're not afraid of you."

Red smiled. "You look like you're terrified. Come on out here and talk to me." Red stuffed his hand into his dirty pocket and dialed the neutron pulse weapon to six. He was done playing games. "Come on out, you flaccid piece of shit."

The young man stepped forward, head thrown back. He gestured left and right to his boys. Red pressed the activator, and the young man shuddered and fell.

"Scared to death. Did I just kill him with my brain? What about you? Anyone else ready to die tonight? Huh?" Red barked. He maintained his distance, but the sudden death of their spokesman left them shocked. "Time to go home, boys."

The ones in the back started to drift away. Red waved them off. He glanced over his shoulder to find the two homeless men standing beside the groceries where he'd put them.

He waited until the last of the gang members had moved away, except for the dead one lying on the sidewalk.

"Come on," he told his new posse. He headed around back and set up a distribution point in the only available light by the garage entrance. As he was passing out food to the orderly queue, the garage door started to rise.

He grabbed the bags and ran for it, then dove into Antony's cesspool. Asheka's limo pulled in, carrying only the driver. The Atchimorian was nowhere to be seen. The limo disappeared underground, and the door closed.

Red resumed his work until everything was given out except for a small protein bar that he kept for himself. He ate it a little at a time.

"Who's going to stay up?" Red asked. A couple emaciated arms rose into the air. "I'd like to get some sleep. Can you wake me if anyone shows up? I'll protect you if you help me."

With a meal in their stomachs, Red wasn't sure they'd remain awake.

"I need three of you to watch in case anything happens. I'll be over here." Red laid down beside Antony's cesspool and closed his eyes. He didn't know why he trusted his new minions, but he did. Still, he kept the neutron pulse weapon in his hand and under his body.

One never knew.

CHAPTER TWELVE

<u>Big Bopper Bistro, a Hotel in Blue Heron</u>

"What did you expect me to do?" Custer raged, angry that his response to the theft had not been something he could take pride in. He had been more than afraid; he had been terrified. Ash and Rivka had made jokes about throwing him out a window, but he didn't see those as real threats.

They stood on the open roof of the building, the most secure location they could find. Rivka trusted nothing about their hotel or Blue Heron.

"You acted how you acted. Change it next time."

"It's that easy for you? I'm processing trauma here, and the best advice you can offer is to fix it."

Rivka glared at him until he backed down. "Here's better advice. Bury that shit deep and take it to your grave. Otherwise, you get to relive it over and over. We provided an example of how you don't embarrass yourself. Do like we did, and that other stuff fades into the distance. Stop processing your trauma, or you'll never get over it."

"I think my trained and licensed therapist would disagree," Custer shot back.

"Your trained and licensed therapist makes his money from your continuous processing. He makes money from treatments, not cures. Look at who benefits to see why a situation has or has not changed. This whole planet is a cesspool. Why is there a drug trade operating out of here at all? What are the benefits?"

"Not all therapists are in it for their own enrichment, just like not all lawyers are in it for that. Why do you do what you do?"

"Justice. I can do something almost no one else is capable of. I absolutely don't do it for personal wealth. I do the job because it needs to be done, and I do it with a clear conscience because I know, beyond a shadow of any doubt, that the perps I convict are guilty. I stand up to them, and that's why, when those scumbags tried to rob us at the restaurant, there was only one way it was going to end."

"Action isn't my thing. I'm a cerebral player." Custer's voice was small and distant. Even he didn't believe in himself anymore. In a matter of two days, Rivka had destroyed his confidence and self-respect.

In Rivka's mind, it needed to be knocked down before it could be built back up, but not as long as he was processing his trauma. She needed him to get past that so he could move forward on a better path. He had been a decent human being at one time. He could be again.

"Your therapist is trying to get you past placing blame since the hardest realization we'll ever have in our lives is that most of the crap that falls on our heads is because of our own decisions. When it's not, that's when we need to talk with someone to get our heads back in the game. Discerning which is which is the challenge. I always assume it's me. Makes it easier to deal with. Then we order All Guns Blazing and eat ourselves silly."

"You don't look like you eat yourself silly. You keep yourself in incredible shape."

"Enhancements, but we work out every day in one way or another. My whole team is in shape for their jobs, even Ankh. After his body was broken and he had to drag himself from Engineering to the Pod-doc, he decided he needed a stronger body to withstand the rigors we put ourselves through. He didn't lament getting busted up. He fixed it and moved on. Just like you need to do, Custer."

"And back to me. Have I been such a failure? Tell me, why was one of your SIs following us? I thought you were going to tell them to stay out of this case."

"While you were in the Pod-doc, I told them exactly that. I don't understand where the wires got crossed, but they keep defying me on this case. I have to get to the bottom of it."

"Maybe they accept that it's far more dangerous than you allow yourself to believe."

Rivka raised an eyebrow. "Sometimes you have incredible insight, but don't let it go to your head."

"Asheka Burako is a cold-hearted killer."

"This I know. And I don't think he'd hesitate to kill us—after trying to do me, of course, and maybe you too. He's all about control. But he's a mini-boss. We want the big guy."

"What if he's not?" Custer wondered. He gazed at the city, bright lights summoning the nightlife by creating it.

"More mad insight from the counselor." Rivka clapped him on the shoulder. "We have to consider that, but we have to keep an open mind, too. If we take him down and he's not the big boss, we'll only strengthen the organization as they learn how to hide from us better. Even if he is the big boss, we still need the rest of the organization. For the record, this undercover work is one and done. We can't shoot this silver bullet again."

Custer shrugged off Rivka's hand and moved away. "I don't want to go undercover again. I just want my corporate office. I want things to go back to the way they were. This was a mistake."

That confirmed Rivka's suspicions.

"You recognize that your life has been forever changed. You know there's no way to go back to business as usual. Why did you accept Grainger's request to join this case?"

"I was hoping working with you would result in something different." He wouldn't look at her. He stared out over the city.

"You hoped I would fall madly in love with the dashing lawyer who deigned to take down the mob. Reality was a cold and wet towel snapping you right in the ass."

He faced her angrily, his lips twisted into a snarl. "That right there. What kind of language is that?"

"Why are you angry about what words I use? Because I'm not like what you imagined me to be? Expectations, Custer. Manage your expectations, and you'll gain control over your life." She crossed her arms and held his gaze. She wouldn't let him return to a fantasy world where she doted on him.

"Be a decent human being just this once. You'll get your

rewards, but they might not be in woman-flesh or precious gems. You'll be able to look at yourself in the mirror because you made the galaxy a better place. It's called your conscience. Feed it and listen to it. Let it fill the spot where your ego used to be since it's going to have to. You can't go back to the way things were."

"Bury the bad memories until the day I die. That's your recipe for a good life?"

"No." Rivka looked at the sky. It was difficult to see the stars with the light pollution of the big city. "It's just life. We can only do our best to live it."

"I understand and think this is the best therapy I'll ever get." Custer headed for the door. "Let's go back inside. There's a floor with pillows on it that's calling my name. I hadn't realized how tired I was. I'm physically and emotionally exhausted. I don't see getting much sleep, but I'll try."

"If you can't sleep, you're not tired enough. That's my answer to insomnia. I don't sleep a whole lot, and my body lets me know. I think I was out for twelve hours when the last case ended. I missed the fresh AGB delivery, and that is the greatest crime that's happened aboard *Wyatt Earp* since the Bad Company took it from the Skaines."

"And to think you mete out Justice with that attitude."

"Awesome, isn't it?" Rivka chuckled. "Burako has no idea what's coming his way. He has his weaknesses, and they are profound. We'll find them, and we'll leverage them."

Chaz walked the streets all night. He had to fend off a number of pickpockets, which was easy since he carried nothing. His sensors told him when an individual was getting handsy.

The last attempt was made by a boy of no more than ten years. "Why do you steal?" Chaz asked.

"Because you have, and I do not."

"I have nothing." Chaz pulled his pockets out to show the boy that they were empty. The boy took the opportunity to feel the material. He didn't trust Chaz to tell him the truth. Satisfied that the pockets were empty, he nodded and started to walk away. Chaz asked, "Would you care to join me for something to eat? I'll buy."

"But you have nothing," the boy countered.

Chaz activated his wink subroutine. The boy chuckled. "You wink funny."

"I'm lucky to wink at all. It's taken me a while to learn these things."

The boy looked at him oddly. "Sure, if you're buying, but not sure how you're going to do that without a credit chip."

"By magic," Chaz replied. He picked a nearby all night diner. He'd already walked past it twice. "Tell me, you're kind of young to be pulling an all-nighter on the streets. Why?"

"My mom's on a medication called Plexorall. It's expensive, so she has to have men over all night, every night. I can't come home until morning because she doesn't want me to know what she does, but I know. There's a chessboard out. She's beating the pants off them for money."

Chaz missed the quadruple entendre, but the meaning was clear. Plexorall. That was the name of the illegal hallucinogen Magistrate Crabbe had found on Delegor. Along with Advantageous, it accounted for the majority of the illegal drugs in the illicit pipelines. Chaz also knew she wasn't playing chess.

"We'll get something good," Chaz promised.

Inside the diner, Chaz had to pre-pay. He waved his wrist over the sensor and covered their impending debt. His SCAMP body had tools not available to the common individual.

The SI had no need to eat, so he fake-sipped his water while he watched the boy and listened to the prepubescent lad's take on the horrors of addiction. He was making the most of it, but that meant theft since he had no role model to show him alternatives.

Chaz did a quick search in the system. He had to hack into the government's main databases, but that was easy since they didn't have an SI fighting to keep people out. Their software was outdated, as was every system that only uploaded patches once a year.

"Have you thought about delivering news bulletins to businesses? How about shelf-stocking, late night shift? It appears there are no child labor laws on this planet."

"You're not from here?" The boy shook his head. "Of course, you're not from here. You'd be really strange if you were."

"Thank you for that. I was going for simply strange. It appears that I have achieved my goal."

The boy laughed and resumed eating. He ate more than someone his age should have, probably to make up for the meals he had missed and for the future ones that wouldn't happen.

"When you're finished, we'll go to the major wholesale house to apply for an overnight position."

"What if I like my life?" the boy asked around a mouth full of food.

"Do you?" Chaz wondered.

He dug into his breakfast without answering. When he finished, Chaz stood. His meal had been boxed.

"Aren't you hungry?"

"No. This is yours for later."

The boy's eyes lit up, but only for a moment. "Are we going for that interview?"

"Yes. We shall see what we can do. I've already applied for you. They're expecting us."

The boy was confused. They left the diner with a wave to the server and hurried down the streets. The warehouse was four blocks away, not far for a brisk walk. The boy kept up with Chaz.

"How do they know we're coming?"

"I'm the magic man. I already told you that."

The boy didn't buy the answer, but Chaz was correct. They were waiting for them and conducted the interview on the spot since the boy's father signed for him. Chaz did it, assessing that the boy would take the real job seriously. After he was shown his assignment and put to work, Chaz met with the administrator.

"What will it take for the boy to move up and be able to provide for his family? His sick mother?"

"Why don't *you* do that?" the other asked sharply. She

had a big, intimidating personality. Chaz saw why people wouldn't cross her.

"Because I'm off-planet way too much and get paid in local currencies. I can't always get it back here when they need it. I'm not a very good father."

"The boy seems like he was raised well. Maybe you're better than you think."

Chaz brightened. "His mother has addiction problems. What kind of resources are available to help?"

The woman shook her head while looking at the floor. "My son, too. There's nothing you can do until they hit rock bottom. Gotta break them first. Three days to break the physical addiction and a lifetime to break the emotional one. You should stay here, even if you have to take a job that pays less."

Chaz calculated the variables in his mind and came to the inevitable conclusion. He needed to get back on the case. "I ship out tonight. I have no choice in the matter, you see. I'm every bit as much a slave to what I do as his mother is to what she does. He'll have to manage it alone, but with this job, he won't be alone."

The administrator glared at Chaz. "That's fucked up."

"You can say that again." He offered his hand, and the administrator shook it half-heartedly. "I have to go."

He left without a word to the boy. There was nothing he could say, but there was something he could do.

CHAPTER THIRTEEN

Wyatt Earp, in Orbit over Delegor

"We need to head down to the planet and arrest Tommy Gamble. He's known in the mob circles as 'Silver Tongue.' Will you join us?" Sahved asked.

Buster's head filled _Wyatt Earp's_ main screen. "I look forward to it. Are we going to include Chief Mak Elb Bint?"

"Delegor's head law enforcement official?" Sahved asked. "We should brief him first, with your concurrence, of course, and lead, as you're the only Magistrate here. We are making believe that Magistrate Rivka is with us."

"I've seen your notes on the case." Buster rotated his shoulders to loosen the muscles in his back. He hadn't realized how tight he was. "Who are we going to arrest if this is a diversion?"

"Whoever the local head is," Sahved replied matter-of-factly. "Make a big show of it, calling him 'Tommy Gamble.'"

"What's that going to do?" Buster wondered. He scratched his head figuratively and literally.

"Divert back to those trying to distract us. They'll be thrown into a state of confusion because they know this is a fake lead. We'll take down the organization that's here."

"We gutted them pretty badly last time I was here," Buster replied. "No, wait. I turned everything over to the local authorities. Son of a bitch!"

"Yes, it would be nice if Rivka was here to see the truth instantly from Chief Mak. We'll have to do it the old-fashioned way." The Yemilorian twirled his three fingers while grinning.

"I always have to do it the old-fashioned way. You guys are spoiled." He stood. "I'll ask Beau to marry airlocks with you, and I'll come over. We can take your ride to the surface. You can turn invisible, can't you?"

"Yes, yes. That's no problem. See you soon, Magistrate." Sahved signed off and jumped out of the captain's seat. Clodagh reached for him but missed. He slammed into the bridge's low ceiling and flopped to the deck, but he quickly stood and dusted himself off. "I meant to do that."

Tiny Man Titan barked once as if he were calling him out.

Sahved looked around as they stood uncomfortably. He wanted to leave, and Clodagh wanted to take the captain's seat for the maneuver to link with Grainger's frigate. She finally gestured at the seat.

Sahved waved and strolled off the bridge, ducking excessively to get through the hatch to the corridor beyond. He would take Dennicron and Lindy with him, but there was only one Magistrate. They'd accompany Buster

Crabbe to the surface and enact Rivka's plan to distract the distractors.

After that, they'd wait for the word on where to go next. They were counting on Rivka to get names and locations. She had a day, no more than two. No one doubted she would get the information.

No one but her.

Baron's Hold, Blue Heron Four

"Ash can't meet with us today, but he requests we join him for dinner," Custer said after checking his communications.

"We needed to talk about some things." Rivka stormed back and forth in the small room, ending by kicking the pillows on the floor into the corner.

Custer had been relegated to the bathroom where he sat on the counter.

"We are at his beck and call. You need more patience. Have you tried meditation?"

"Meditation! Ha. I tried it, and it nearly drove me insane. Not going to do it again. Sit and do nothing? I can't do that. It's the express elevator to hell."

Custer threw up his hands. Being stuck in a room with a stir-crazy Magistrate wasn't his idea of a good time.

"I'm going out." Custer did his best to sound confident.

"Where?"

"Who died and left you in charge of me? I'm going out to refill my soul after you sucked it dry."

"I shined the spotlight on the darkness within, you fucking wanksplat. Where are you going?"

"The concierge. I'm going to ask them what there is to do if one has the day free. Maybe there's an amusement park. We can catch a roller coaster or something." Custer hopped down, took one step, and reached for the door handle. He stopped and looked over his shoulder. "Coming?"

"I guess." Rivka surrendered to the suggestion since she had no ideas. She was stuck in an endless loop of wanting to continue her verbal jousting with Burako until he revealed something important. Then she'd take him down, along with his whole organization. That would have to wait. "Looks like we're going to an amusement park. Hopefully, no one tries to rob us while we're there."

"Get robbed once, and you're all gun-shy about going out. I don't even know if there is a park. We'll find out shortly." Custer opened the door.

Rivka resigned herself to the fate of spending the day with someone she didn't want to spend the day with, doing things she considered unproductive. *Undercover,* she reminded her workaholic self. *Do nothing and like it.*

Wyatt Earp, Landing Pad on the Outskirts of Batik Magal, Delegor

"We go in guns blazing. *Blam, blam, kapow*! We mow them down, blow the smoke from the barrels, and stroll away, our spurs tinkling like angels' bells," Buster said.

"What?" Sahved didn't get any of the references.

"Let's not and say we did," Lindy replied in a glum voice.

"I had to try it. Don't you people get into the old Wyatt

Earp spirit? He was a lawman, after all, with a reputation for shooting first and asking questions later." Buster was doing all the talking, and the team wasn't responding. "This is my first time on board your ship."

"It's quite a ship," Sahved stated.

Lindy stared at the deck. She kept her hand near the big red button, ready to push it in her husband's place.

Sahved moved in front of the hatch and raised his hands for silence, even though no one was making a sound. "We are doing Rivka's bidding. As much as we don't want to do it with teammates, friends, and family missing, we have to. Rivka asked us to. We stand in her stead. It is for us to bring this part of the case to fruition. The mob must believe we are wrongly barking at the right tree."

Tyler was watching from the back of the group. "That's it exactly." He thumped his body armor. "I'm no Vered the Mighty, but I'll do my best." He tapped Rivka's railgun, which Red had named Ethel.

Lindy saluted with her railgun, taking care not to hit anyone. Her finger was outside the trigger guard, lying along the frame to prevent accidental discharges.

Sahved pointed at Buster. "Magistrate Crabbe, take the lead."

"By the power invested in me by High Chancellor Wyatt and the Federation, I accept your challenge to arrest everyone." He made a fist and shook it in front of himself.

"What?" Sahved wondered. "I am still having a hard time understanding human humor. You people are weird."

"Thank you." Buster was so used to being alone that he wasn't sure how to deal with a team. "I'm doing my best. Our first order of business is to meet with Chief Mak Elb

Bint. He will brief us on the extent of his investigation, and then we'll pull the trigger and go after those he's identified as players in the drug-smuggling business."

Buster executed an about-face, then pointed a knife hand at the hatch. Lindy hit the button, both hatches opened, and the stairs descended. Lindy tried to get in front of Buster, but he strode off in a hurry. He wore an amulet around his neck. It was a comm link through *Wyatt Earp* to Philko, who was halfway across the galaxy.

Outside, Lindy caught up with Buster. "I go first, so no one shoots you."

"That doesn't happen." Buster saw that she was serious. "Does it?"

"At least twice, probably more. First blood on one case was something like four seconds. Rivka got shot in the chest. We've modified our procedures since then. Red always goes first and blocks the view of her with his body."

"He's been shot." Buster slowed down.

"A lot of times. We all have. It's part of the job."

"Reading Rivka's case files is like reading a thriller novel. I reconcile myself with the danger by believing it's fiction. My cases are almost all white-collar crimes. They don't require warriors in full combat gear."

"We have them on backup. Cole and his team are one call away from a high-speed insert."

"You guys don't mess around." Buster sized up Rivka's team. "Are you upset because Red's not here, or is it Rivka?"

The waiting van had one occupant. Chief Mak.

"It's Dery. He saw something with Red. A trial by fire, he called it. I don't know what that means, but it made him sad, and that upsets me a whole lot." Lindy's eyes kept moving, raking the area for threats. Throwing herself into her job helped allay the anxiety gnawing on her insides.

Mak stepped out and greeted his friend Buster. Lindy and Tyler turned their backs on the group and watched for anything that needed to be seen. The others huddled around the chief.

"These are trying times," Buster started. "With focus and diligence, we will gut the planet's smugglers and drug trade. I have high expectations, Mak."

"As do I. You sent me a hard question that I didn't answer." Mak leaned back when Sahved loomed over him, listening intently. "You asked why haven't I acted since you were last here. The Delegador has been dragging his feet, but I haven't been pushing as hard as I could. I think there might be corruption in the higher levels of the government."

Buster looked at Sahved. "I'll see the Delegador and start that chain of inquiry. You and Dennicron go with Mak and lead the parade of suspects to the hoosegow."

"'Hoosegow' is a word that is so very much unknown to me. Does that mean a place of worship?"

Buster turned his head one way and then another as if looking to see if he was being secretly recorded. "It's not a house of worship. Where do you usually take suspects?"

"They should find a higher calling to lead them from their lives of crime. I think we should take them to the celestial temple and start them chanting for redemption."

"I thought Rivka worked outside the box," Buster mumbled. "It's all of you. Hoosegow is a jail but in cool Wyatt Earp-era terms."

"I live in the Wyatt Earp era and have never ever in all the time of my existence heard that term."

"Not this *Wyatt Earp*. The other one." Buster sized up the Yemilorian. "You win. Take them to the local jail. I'll have Philko arrange for transport off-planet."

"We can do that!" Sahved beamed. Lindy shrugged. Dennicron nodded, and Tyler shook his head.

"Beau, get me an immediate appointment with the Delegador, and I mean immediate."

Mak watched, fascinated, like a morbid voyeur. It was a trainwreck about which he could do nothing except wait until it ended to clean up the mess.

Confirmed, Beau replied.

"Drop me off at the Delegador's offices. You guys continue on to the law enforcement center so you can arrange the mass pick-up. I'll catch up with you."

Mak looked away.

Buster caught his expression. The Magistrate ushered the team into the van. "Don't tell me; let me guess. You don't have any leads."

Mak brightened. "We have leads, but they're not very good."

"Maybe we're the ones who need to retire to a house of worship." Buster was the second-last to board. Mak was the last one in. The door closed, and the vehicle raced away. It had lights and a siren. That wasn't what the group wanted, but Mak smiled. He seemed to enjoy the domination it gave the driver over the traffic. The other vehicles pulled out of the way as the van zoomed through.

No one spoke during the trip to the Delegador's building. The van pulled up out front, and Buster climbed out.

He shook hands with Mak and walked toward the familiar building. Mak stepped back into the van and turned to Sahved. "We have one lead that's very good. We shall visit him first. An individual from Foromme named Chloral Mist."

Sahved looked at Dennicron to determine if they had anything on that individual. She accessed her internal files before connecting to *Wyatt Earp* and getting help from Clevarious. "It'll be a few minutes," she announced.

"A few minutes for what?" Mak wondered.

"We are researching everything the Federation knows about an individual named Chloral Mist."

Mak studied the team members. No one looked different besides Sahved. The others were unremarkably human. "How?"

Dennicron explained in some detail what a SCAMP was.

The chief followed her explanation. "I've never met an SI before."

Dennicron nodded politely. She had nothing else to say. He had met one now, and it changed nothing.

Sahved said, "This Chloral Mist. What evidence do you have? Can we leverage her for greater information?"

Mak shrugged a non-answer. "We'll take our best shot."

"Maybe we'll get nothing and like it," the dentist suggested from the last seat.

"Possibly." Mak seemed open to not making an arrest.

Sahved wasn't having it. "We must make an arrest. It's why we're here. Whoever we arrest, we will call them "Silver Tongue." We will announce it publicly but not show the face."

"Why do we want to go public? Every other part of the organization will know you're lying."

"Will they?" Sahved wasn't sure. "They'll wonder what they don't know. They will realize they've been lied to or kept in the dark, right where we want them. Contact Flight Control and let them know we're putting an orbital stop on all newly arriving transport and cargo ships."

Mak frowned. "I'm not sure we want to do that."

"We're going to do that." Sahved gave the chief no choice. "It's part of the bigger plan."

"You have a bigger plan? Can you tell me what it is?"

Sahved shook his head.

"That's odd. I thought we were working together." Mak leaned back in his seat and stared out the window.

The Yemilorian had no problem stonewalling the chief. It was part of the plan since they didn't know who they could trust. People from Delegor and Foromme had proven untrustworthy in the past. Buster had cultivated a relationship with the leadership, but Rivka and her crew had not. *Trust no one on that planet*, Rivka had warned.

"You have a most beautiful planet that is more beautiful than any other planet I have visited ever in my whole life."

Lindy drew a line across her neck when the chief wasn't looking. She implored Sahved to stop talking, but he had grown nervous. He had only been in charge of an investigation once before. He wasn't comfortable with this one. If they were to trust no one, who were they going to arrest?

Would they have to release this person later, or would the locals take care of him? Too many unanswered questions.

"I want to stop by the office first," Mak said.

He had said that before. "I would like it if we didn't," Sahved replied.

"I prefer we do."

Lindy eased into the conversation. "I think it best we go straight to the perp's location before they get wind we're coming. We can't protect anyone if they start scrambling. Heaven forbid they're armed. We don't want to kill anyone. Not today."

"Or any day," Sahved added with a vigorous nod.

Mak seemed put out. "We'll go there, but be advised that we won't have backup."

"We'll call for backup once we are on site. We will assess while backup is on its way." Sahved was doing his best to contain the engagement. A perp, packaged for delivery. It seemed too easy, but the chief had reservations. What didn't he know, or what did he know that he wasn't sharing?

Lindy picked up on it all. Mak seemed less defensive when he was talking with her. "Why the reluctance? We'll make it quick and as painless as possible. We want to talk with this individual, but we also need a bit of a show."

"I don't understand any of this," Mak replied. "We're in a hurry, but it's all for show? I can't have my department used like this." He ordered the driver to the station.

Dennicron had hacked into the self-driving mode. She took control of the vehicle.

The driver let Mak know he was no longer in control.

"You're kidnapping me?"

"That wasn't our first choice. We'll call it 'taking you into custody pending our investigation into corruption at

Delegor's senior leadership levels,'" Sahved explained with exceptional savvy. He had his moments.

Mak fumed, glaring at the Yemilorian, who appeared unfazed by the change of circumstances. Inside, he fought the turmoil of thinking he was doing it all wrong. It wasn't going as he'd expected.

Lindy nudged him and gave him the thumbs-up.

"Next stop, Chloral Mist. Where is he, and what does the facility or residence look like?" Sahved asked.

Mak gave him the finger. He closed his eyes and pulled his hat over his face.

"This is going to be fun," Tyler mumbled from the back.

CHAPTER FOURTEEN

<u>The Mid-Rise Tower, Baron's Hold, Blue Heron Four</u>

Red opened his eyes and immediately checked for Reaper. The small weapon was in his pocket, and his hand was firmly on it. He looked around to find that the sun had risen. The homeless had found places to relax and rest. One was awake. Her bloodshot eyes stared at him from sunken sockets.

He stood and stretched. "Thank you, all of you," he said loudly.

"Do you have any more food?" they asked, although they'd eaten it all the night before. They knew what he'd had. Their question was whether he could get more.

"I might be able to find some," he told them.

They had nothing else to say. Their lives were the simplest of the simple. Find food. Rest.

"Has a vehicle come out of the garage?" Red wondered. One head shook, then another. It hadn't left after last night's late return. How did the younger Burako get to work? "Antony, are you up?"

"What's wrong with you, making all that noise during my prime sleep time?"

"Get up, you lazy bastard," Red told him. He reached in to clear trash from one of Anthony's feet, then gripped the ankle and dragged him out. "I need a hand getting some more food."

"I'm busy," the old man snapped, running his hand through greasy strands of hair.

"Are not. We're going on a quest to help these people."

"Why them and not me?"

"What the fuck is wrong with you, Antony? You'll get yours, too. When one wins, we all win. That includes you. Get your ass up."

"Feed me once, and you think we're engaged? How about you kiss my ass?"

"You smell like ass. There's no kissing in our future. My wife wouldn't approve."

"You said she left you."

"I hope to get her back. That won't happen if I taste like you."

The grind of the garage door opening announced the imminent departure of a vehicle. The limo appeared when the gate rose and slowly drove away.

"What do you think that's about?" Red asked his offal-smelling partner.

"He's going to pick up my no-good son."

"The limo driver lives here, but Ash does not. Where does he live, and does he conduct any business out of his house?"

"Them's some pointed questions, the likes of which get a man in trouble."

"Maybe I've had it with drug dealers ruining people's lives, like mine, and I'm going to speak my piece to them, starting with this one. How long before he returns?"

"At least an hour. Always at least an hour. It's like Ash makes him wait to show him who's in charge."

"Or the driver goes early to make sure he's on time, whatever 'on time' means." Red gestured at the side street. "We can get out, buy some grub, and get back before the man returns. Then maybe we'll go in there and have a few words."

"How are you going to get past Hex?"

"The Atchimorian? Those guys are like My Little Ponies, all fluff and glitter. I'll kick his ass before he knows he's been in a fight."

"I don't think you've ever fought an Atchimorian before," Antony said. "But you seem crazy enough to give it a try. I'll watch for posterity's sake, so I can tell the meat wagon when it shows up to drag your carcass away. I'll do that for you because I like you."

Red clapped the old man on the back. It was like slapping a bistok pie. There was a wet slop. Red pulled his hand back and bent over to wipe it on the ground. "Why do you sleep in a cesspool?"

"Because no one will take it from me."

A straightforward answer. Red thought the old man had hit rock bottom. There was nowhere lower. His only relief came from the comfort that he had nothing else to take away.

"We'll see what we can do," Red promised, being intentionally vague. His ire rose. How could a son do something like this to his dad? Red wanted to extract a pound of flesh from Burako and his muscle for the injustices that had been perpetrated on the few people Red had met.

He blinked away the smell of the alley behind the mid-rise tower. This was Rivka's case, and he was there to protect her. He had to wait for her to give the order to take down the perps. If he did it early, her case would be blown.

"We'll watch first, and in due time, we'll deliver the beat-down that will change the trajectory of your son's career."

"I can't wait to see that. You said something about food. I haven't had breakfast in a silver moon. This could be a banner day. Do you have anything on you?"

"No, old man. We have to go get it. I might have a credit chip with a few credits on it. We'll see what the store has to say." Red walked ahead. Antony Burako stood where he was. He crossed his arms and became belligerent. "Now what?"

"Who do you think you are to order me around?"

"If you go with me, you can choose what you want. If you don't, you'll get a fish head and maybe some gum off my boot."

The old man snorted. "That's the spirit. Make it worth my time. I'll go with you, you bastard."

Red walked ahead. It was up to the old man to catch up. He wanted to be back for Ash's return. He wanted to be up on the twenty-first floor in a place where he could learn what he needed for when the time came to act. Maybe he'd take Antony so he'd have a reason to be there. Ratchet up the confrontation without including the Magistrate.

"Bastard," Red reiterated.

. . .

Blue Heron

Chaz wandered aimlessly while engaging digitally with anything he could connect to. He scanned the networks for information and found much. He parsed it all and created a concise report of places he thought were laundering money, along with the names of those doing the laundering, for Rivka.

He wished he could vet the information and share it with the Magistrate. He wanted to move forward with the case. His Good Samaritan efforts during the previous night had been useful as a distraction, and he didn't know why, but they had made him feel good. That wasn't something he was used to, although he'd been developing his emotions for years. He was not yet comfortable with what they meant, though. He didn't want to risk feeling wrong.

It dawned on him that he was one of Rivka's investigators, but that wasn't limited to digital work. He decided to visit one of the money launderers to see if he could start unraveling tendrils of the mob and, most importantly, find a direct link to Asheka Burako.

The coin-operated laundromat on the edge of the downtown didn't look like it should turn a profit of a hundred thousand credits a month. Not that it could. Quick math suggested if every machine was running every hour of every day of the month, the total revenue before expenses would barely be thirty thousand.

When Chaz walked down the row of machines, half of them were out of order. Some were filled with water. Some were missing doors. Fifteen thousand if the operable ones were running, and they weren't. One washer was running, the machine next to the one small table and credit exchange. A small individual sat behind it, reading a spread-out newspaper.

"Good afternoon," Chaz started, standing casually.

The newspaper came down slowly. The face was ancient. The individual wasn't a teenager as Chaz had first thought, but someone who had left their best days behind them. Chaz wondered if she had ever had good days.

"It's not hard. Present your credit chip and get a card for however many loads you want to do. It's two for drying. Electricity has gone way up in price."

Chaz ignored the directions, assuming she hadn't noticed that he carried no laundry. "Are you the proprietor?"

"Yeah. That's me. Pure wealth right here. What's it to you?"

Chaz wasn't going to get anywhere by taking it easy. She started to raise her newspaper. "You are claiming one hundred thousand credits a month in revenue. That is demonstrably false, which means you are running a money laundering operation. That is illegal, a felony on Blue Heron Four."

She lowered the newspaper, scrunching her face to get a good look at Chaz. "You don't look like the cops."

"I'm much worse. I'm an investigator, and you're busted."

She raised her newspaper. "I'm not. And you can't get free laundry. One credit to wash. Two to dry. If you're not doing any loads, then be on your way. I run a respectable business."

"That is not true." Chaz reached out and lowered the newspaper with one finger. He found himself staring into the oversized barrel of a homemade weapon not unlike the one the Magistrate had liberated from the people who had attempted to rob Bangers.

"If I blow you away, then I have to clean up the mess. I'm going to set the record straight first. I run a clean business. Look at me. You think I'm laundering money? Ain't happening. I wouldn't be sitting here if I had the kind of scratch you're talking about. Now, get out of here, and I won't call the cops on you."

Chaz used SCAMP speed to rip through the newspaper and twist the pistol out of the old woman's grasp. Before she could take her next breath, Chaz had tossed the disassembled weapon into the nearest washer that was filled with water.

"Who do you report to?"

"I have a business accountant. All of us do. He doesn't charge anything, so I don't ask any questions."

"Name and address of this accountant, please."

She gave him the name of one Bankshot McCoy. If Chaz had been human, he would have blinked at the ridiculous name. As it was, he accepted the name on the face of it and the address, which was only ten blocks away. He touched his brow in a salute and walked out. The woman had no idea who he was, and he'd gotten potentially valuable information. He had double-checked that the business was legitimate, but it wasn't rolling the kind of numbers that suggested it was doing the accounting for million-credit businesses.

An accountant to the mob, Chaz thought. He smiled internally while maintaining a slightly angry expression, which he had calculated would keep the pickpockets and other criminal elements away from him. His sensors would tell him when he needed to run off the ones who got too close.

It was always younger kids. They bothered him more than he could allow. He tucked the information away and returned his attention to Mister McCoy.

With his rapid walk, he covered the long ten blocks in twenty minutes. When he reached the office, they were just shutting off the lights and preparing to leave. Chaz waited for the proprietor and a secretary to step into the corridor. When the door behind them was secured, Chaz approached.

"Why are you leaving so early in the day?" Chaz asked.

The man tensed while sizing up Chaz. He relaxed and answered, "Today was a day off, but we came in anyway because we work too hard. That's what it takes to run a successful business."

"Let's go into your office so we can talk about how you're laundering money. The laundromat is just one such business, but I suspect there are at least six more. This isn't a conversation for the corridor, talking about your felonies. Please, unlock your door, and let's talk like civilized people."

The man wasn't used to being confronted, which explained why he was running. The laundromat's proprietor had alerted him, but he had been too slow in leaving because Chaz had walked much faster than they'd estimated. He fiddled with his briefcase.

"If you pull a weapon out of there, I'll break both your arms, and then we'll still have the conversation. Do you want to do it with pain or without? The choice is yours, Bankshot."

"She's Bankshot. I'm McCoy." He nodded at the woman. Chaz didn't take his eyes off the man.

"Please." Chaz gestured at the office again.

McCoy dropped his chin to his chest and stumbled back to the office. He opened it with a hand print and a retina scan, two technologies that were cutting edge for Blue Heron Four. The planet was backward.

Chaz tried breaking into their computer systems the second they walked into the office, but they were physically turned off, which was the safest security in the galaxy. "You'll need to power up your computer systems."

"No way. You'll need a subpoena or something for that."

"A subpoena? You are misguided in your understanding of who I am." Chaz moved a chair that placed him close to the door with his back to the wall. The two accountants were trapped in the office. "Who are you laundering money for?"

They looked at each other, crossed their arms in unison, and clamped their mouths shut until their lips turned white.

"Nice try. I'm going to restrain you, and then I'm going to power up your systems, access what I need, and copy it all. Then I'll tell all of Blue Heron Four you can't be trusted to keep their secrets."

The man got angry and came out of his seat, but Chaz was faster. He stiff-armed him in the chest and drove him back into his chair. "You might as well kill us yourself."

"I get it. You work for bad people. If you want those bad

people to go away, I'll do it without all the publicity. I promise you."

The man snorted, then braced his elbows on his knees and rested his face in his hands. He breathed deeply and regularly as if he were practicing a calming technique.

"A promise you may or may not keep. I don't know you from anyone. All I know is that you've put us at great risk."

"Ah, yes. You might think that, but you put yourselves at risk by getting your hands dirty. You're upset because you've been caught. It is the way of things that criminals inevitably get caught and punished for their crimes. I believe the proper saying is, 'It's time to pay the piper.'"

Chaz waited for a few moments, letting silence raise the anxiety of the two being questioned. "But with a little cooperation, your involvement could be minimized."

"We're done. If we give you anything, they'll find us. Why are you doing this? If you aren't the cops, then who are you?"

Chaz decided to steal a line from the Bad Company. "I'm a member of a private conflict resolution enterprise. A friend of mine, a young boy, has to work nights because his mom is hooking to pay for her drug habit. I'm not good with that, so I'm going to take down the entire drug ring infesting this planet."

"That's a big ask. I don't think one person can do it."

"You need to listen better if you're to have any hope of surviving this."

The pair kept their mouths shut.

"Now that I have your attention, stand up and turn around." The two complied. Chaz used electrical cords to bind their hands, then pushed them back into their seats backward, facing the wall.

A quick look showed him the power system for the computers, a server and two workstations. He booted the server, then brought up both workstations. Everything was password protected, but they also had a biometric component. The good news was that Chaz had access to the two people who were keyed into the system. He yanked McCoy around until he could jam his hand on the pad.

It required a password, but the system was working and active. Chaz was quick to find a back door and entered the computer.

"Look at all these spreadsheets and databases. You even keep track of how much product is pushed. Look at those delivery planets. My. I think this is all we're going to need."

"You can't possibly be in the system," McCoy groused. Chaz turned the two around to face him and one of the workstations. Without looking at the computer, Chaz gestured like a magician, then bowed from the waist. The login screen disappeared and the system started scrolling through the files, bringing up random spreadsheets and magnifying cells with key data before moving on. "How are you doing this?"

"How doesn't matter. You're in big trouble. The firm of Bankshot McCoy is effectively shut down as of this moment. How do you want to play this?"

"What are our options?" Bankshot asked after a sigh that signaled her surrender.

"You would have had more had you been forthcoming from the outset. But since you forced me to play hardcore badminton, you'll answer all my questions. Then we'll explore more options. I want restitution and a return to peace for my young friend. I want him to sleep at home at night and his mom not to have to work."

"We can make that happen. A living stipend. She can be free to explore other pursuits without having to worry about money," McCoy offered.

"Yes, but no. You see, that won't do since there are a lot of distraught mothers out there. Here's what I need you to do. Give me the names of the dealers and the one calling the shots. That's the starting point. Everything else will flow from that information."

Chaz continued to download their files. The archives were extensive, and the working files were enough to buy them serious time in Jhiordaan if the Magistrate saw it all and extrapolated the number of lives ruined.

It might rise to the level of a capital crime.

"I'll show you, but you need to untie me."

"Really?" Chaz ran his laugh subroutine, then replayed it to double the effect.

The duplicate laugh tracks unnerved the two prisoners.

"What are you?" Bankshot asked.

"A higher form of life. I'm this little guy driving this big body around. I'm in here pulling levers with a massive stogie torched and smoking. Can't you smell it?"

There was nothing to smell, but Chaz wanted to get into their heads and unseat them from reality.

They both sniffed. "I don't smell anything." Bankshot shook her head.

"Your loss," Chaz countered. "Now, I'm going to need those names."

He untied Bankshot, opting to leave the one who was

more likely to be aggressive restrained. McCoy was destined to watch.

She opened a drawer in her desk and removed a pad and pen. She wrote one name at the top, then drew six lines and listed six more names. Beneath those were three additional names. She handed the paper to the SI.

"There you go."

The name at the top was enlightening.

Asheka Burako.

"Where do these underlings work?"

She started naming planets. Six main planets and eighteen subordinate planets.

"Who's in charge of Blue Heron Four?"

She pointed at one of the six. "Pantone Martini."

"Is that a real name? I thought Bankshot McCoy was a porn star. I think you two are making stuff up, buying time until an accomplice arrives. Do you have a hidden panic button? Well, do you?"

Chaz had disabled it when they'd entered the room. They had cutting-edge technology but weren't using it to its full capability. It was doubtful they knew how to use it at all, simply buying and installing what they thought they needed.

You should have invested in an SI. Then I wouldn't have found you, and we wouldn't be here. Except we would because the Singularity isn't going to knowingly assist in a crime like this. Oh, well. You lose, Chaz thought. He maintained his neutral external expression in a way a warm-blooded creature couldn't. There were no tells to give away his internal thoughts if he didn't activate a subroutine.

Chaz casually reached under the desk he thought was

McCoy's and ripped the button off. He showed it to both of them. "This was disabled when you pushed it on your way to sit down. So, now that I've crushed your spirit, thinking that someone is going to come and save you, are you going to help me?"

The two looked at each other once more.

"I figured it didn't work since they should have been here already. The response team is in this building. They'll check on us anyway. Maybe we can hold out."

"Maybe you can. Let's wait and see." Chaz leaned against the wall, keeping an eye on the entrance and also on those in his charge. He continued to process the information he'd pulled from their computer system, consolidating and building an organizational chart. The Magistrate would want to know that she was trying to infiltrate from the very top.

He tried to contact her on her comm chip, but she didn't reply. On a low-tech world like Blue Heron Four, he should have had sufficient range unless the building's materials were of the type that would stymy a signal. Or maybe she had deactivated her chip, as they'd done to Red's.

Whatever the reason, Chaz was alone. There was no sympathetic SI running the planetary systems he could tap to contact *Wyatt Earp* to deliver his information and get help.

Dennicron would have been a good sounding board. He made a note to develop a portable Instantaneous Intergalactic Comm terminal in case they were ever separated again, one they could access using their comm chips. Then they would never be out of contact. Blue Heron Four didn't have an IIC terminal. They had to communicate the old-fashioned way, through the Gate when it was active, using burst transmissions.

How barbaric, Chaz thought in a brief moment of mirth before he returned to his current need. He wanted them to share what they knew beyond what he found on their computer systems. There was always something unwritten, and it was inevitably of vital importance.

"Here's what I'm going to do. I'll create a line and block diagram of the illicit trade you've been supporting, based on what I've found in your computer."

Chaz found their use of a whiteboard quaint, even though the information on it listed restaurants and hours and all manner of things that had no bearing on what he was doing. He did catalog the information for future use.

He started at the top with Burako and drew three lines. He added the names and planets. He pointed behind him. "Don't move."

His sensors had detected McCoy trying to ease toward his computer.

"How do you know all this? Are you wired?"

Chaz turned around, covered his ear with a hand, and whispered, "What should I tell them? Really? Okay." He uncovered his ear. "They said to tell you no."

He returned to the board and continued drawing. One tendril was nothing but Blue Heron Four, but the others expanded across the galaxy. At the bottom, what should have been a minor player, four levels down from the boss, was a name and the planet Yoll.

"My, my," Chaz said. "This is most disconcerting. You've gotten your hooks into Yoll. And what is this we have on

Delegor?" Two down from the top, the single name was Philagaster. "Who would this person be?" Chaz pointed while looking at the two in his charge.

They wouldn't meet his eyes. He could stare without blinking, which most humans found unsettling. These two weren't going to fall into the trap. Not again, anyway. They knew they couldn't outstare him.

"We might have gotten off on the wrong foot." Chaz smiled pleasantly. "Your business is done, but if you walk out of here with a chance to disappear before Mister Burako finds you, that's another question. The current answer isn't looking good."

"You can't get us off this planet without him knowing."

"You underestimate my abilities. We can and will get you off this planet, but only if you cooperate. Everything I have so far I have taken from you. How about you start thinking about saving yourselves if not the untold number of lives these businesses negatively impact? I implore you."

Chaz liked his use of the word "implore" since he'd never used it before. He'd also never injected humor into an interrogation as he had in this one. He couldn't wait to tell Dennicron about "They said to tell you no." He thought that was the work of a genius.

Now if he could only contact the Magistrate and *Wyatt Earp*.

CHAPTER FIFTEEN

<u>Entertainment Complex, Blue Heron</u>

"This sucks hairy meatballs," Rivka complained.

"You have to learn how to relax," Custer countered. "Maybe it's you who sucks."

"Pretty sure it's not." Rivka glanced around the area for a distraction while they killed time until their so-called dinner engagement, Round Two.

The concierge had directed them to a well-kept but aging circus next to a shopping mall. There were no live acts except with domesticated animals. The Federation had outlawed such things to interdict any interplanetary trade in exotic life forms.

The smell of bistok wafted past them. It was of an intensity that made them choke. Rivka headed toward the mall and better ventilation.

"Smells like money," Custer wheezed out, gasping.

Rivka slowed down. She was quickly growing accustomed to the stench, which was probably her enhancements kicking in to fight it off. Custer rushed ahead.

That made it worthwhile for Rivka. She hoped the smell wouldn't penetrate her clothes. She thought she might keep them after this case rather than recycle them into something else. Rivka found Custer's discomfort to be relaxing despite knowing she shouldn't.

Rivka caught up with him inside the entrance to the shopping mall. The air was distinctly different, well-filtered and cool.

"Much better than the stockyard, don't you think?" Custer raised his eyebrows and smiled as if he were Rivka's savior.

"I'll remind you that it was your choice to visit said stockyard. Do you see any people using electronics?" It was a rhetorical question. From the browsers to the systems within the stores, it was one of the most modern facilities Rivka had seen since her arrival.

Custer spread his arms wide. "Everywhere."

Rivka activated her comm chip. *Red? Chaz? Are you guys where you can talk?*

She didn't hold out hope that she would get a reply, but Chaz surprised her with his instantaneous answer.

I'm glad you're there. I have info on the entire organization. Not just Blue Heron Four but this entire sector of space, all the way to Yoll.

Rivka turned away and leaned her head on the wall. *All the way to Yoll? Do you have names?*

Asheka Burako is in charge of it all, Magistrate.

Rivka raised her head and glared at the still-smiling Atticus Tikabow. She grabbed him by the arm. "Did you know that Ash is in charge of it all?"

He'd suspected but hadn't opened his mouth since he

knew that he didn't have to. Fear crept across his face like a slow-moving train wreck.

Rivka continued, "How did you think you could hide that from me?"

"I figured you'd learn it instantly from him, and you'd take him down before he could retaliate. I didn't think you'd drag this thing out while simultaneously making me the butt of your derision." Anger replaced fear, but it quickly subsided. Custer had a weak play, and he knew it.

"I'll deal with you later. We'll take Ash down at dinner." She switched to her comm chip. *Where are you, Chaz, and have you heard from Red?*

I'm at the accountants' office. The ones who are laundering the money here on Blue Heron Four but advising others elsewhere. This is the home of it. I think they are planning to move their base of operations. Blue Heron Four has become unstable.

You can say that again. Is it because of the drugs? Rivka caught a whiff of the outside odor. It didn't smell like money to her, but it could be. Water and grass were all bistok needed to flourish. If they weren't going to eat it, they could export it.

Yes. They've gutted this planet and are moving to a more lucrative target. Chaz had no emotion in his voice. He was simply conveying what he had learned.

Funny how that works. We'll have scores of addicts without a supply. That'll be an industry unto itself, but that's going to happen sooner rather than later. We're meeting Burako for dinner. I'll personally take him down. I wish Wyatt Earp was here so I could look at all the information and make a final judgment. Death is probably too good for him, but it would decapitate the organization and cut off their process, at least temporarily. I want the whole thing.

I have the next four levels down, complete with names.

That got Rivka's attention. *Get that to Grainger! Let's get them all at once, coordinated for four hours from now.*

How? Chaz asked a simple question, but it had profound implications.

Rivka looked at Custer for an answer. "Time to start redeeming yourself. How did you get information off-planet when you visited?"

"From the transport ship's business suite once we were in orbit and headed for the open Gate."

"You didn't talk to your office at all while you were here?"

Custer shrugged with wide eyes. "We could send emails, but they would go into the public packet consolidation for burst through the Gate the next time it was open. It's how the rest of the universe works, Rivka."

"It's not how the rest of the universe works, Asswipe." Rivka glared. *We'll have to send an email. Can you do it from where you are?*

How quaint! Chaz replied. *I'll encrypt it for Singularity decoding in a special dispatch for the embassy. They can get it to Grainger.*

Do we know when the next Gate transfer will take place? Ankh would tear apart Rivka's question. She wanted to know when the Gate would next open, not whether Chaz knew the information.

Four hours, Magistrate.

Send it with all the information you have, Rivka ordered. *Add that I will take down Asheka Burako in six hours. That means they have two hours to get their shit together. He gets taken down tonight, especially since his accountants are in our custody. They are in our custody, aren't they?*

I have them both right here. They are not singing like canaries, but they don't need to. They will be forthcoming. Silence followed, then Chaz continued. *It's good to hear from you, Magistrate. I've never been completely alone before.*

First time for everything. How did you get there?

I walked, Chaz replied.

Rivka closed her eyes. *I mean, how did you find the accountants? That sounds like a wild stroke of luck that's too good to be true. It makes me suspicious.*

I availed myself of the planet's financial transaction system, which is deplorably insecure. Money laundering was obvious, using the parameters we learned aboard Wyatt Earp. *I visited a laundromat and then came here. They have great security but don't know how to use it. If they had installed it properly, I would not have what I have.*

Rivka tried to remember if she'd prepared a search warrant for leads related to drug smuggling. Even if she had, hacking into the planet's financial systems was probably fruit of the poisoned tree. She put on her Magistrate hat to defend the action as being in the best interests of the entire planet.

She was operating outside the law to justify a means to an end that would benefit the Federation. Taking down the mob and their burgeoning drug trade was as high a priority as stopping a war between planets. Thanks to Nefas' interference, the mob hadn't grown like they wanted. After he was out of the way, they had jumped into the void.

The Federation would approve it because Rivka had. *Post hoc ergo propter hoc* was a fallacy. Just because something happened, it wasn't necessarily caused by the first thing. Innocent until proven guilty. The result does not detail the cause, but Rivka embraced it as her mind whirled through the legal machinations and arguments she would have to make if she was hauled before the Federation Council.

Because the planet was degrading so quickly, there had to be an external cause that validated the search of Blue Heron Four's financial systems. The fact that money laundering was discovered, Rivka assumed quickly and easily, showed that Blue Heron Four had failed in protecting itself and its citizens. She'd have to meet with the planet's leadership after the suspects were in custody.

Suspects. She trusted the information. Burako wasn't a suspect. He was a criminal and soon to be convicted by a Magistrate. Punishment would depend on whether he resisted.

She expected she would have to kill him and had reconciled herself to that.

"Why didn't Burako have security at the restaurant? You'd think someone of his importance would never be the target of petty crime." It was as if Custer were reading her thoughts, but he was thinking of the case, too, and Asheka's part in it.

"Maybe it was us," Rivka replied. "He didn't want to appear like he was putting on airs. You saw that he was not afraid. He had no intention of putting a credit chip out there for the thug to grab. That guy only looked at you. Maybe it was a setup, once again for our benefit, to make you think exactly like that. Crime bosses don't get hit by burglars."

"No fear because there would be no retaliation. Maybe those two didn't know the big guy would be there." Custer seemed to be delaying.

Rivka walked away. "I'm going back to the hotel. You can sniff bistok butts if you want."

"I came to the mall because bistok butt is not something I ever want to smell again." He pointed in the opposite direction, away from the so-called circus. "We can catch a cab on the other side."

Rivka capitulated. She didn't care where she caught the cab. They had plenty of time. She needed to think, so she planned on sending Custer to the pool while she contemplated the legal ramifications of their actions, both past and future.

She never knew when or who would ask the questions, but being ready had helped her stay in her position. Doing right by the Federation was a higher calling she had to answer for every day of her life.

Every day was hard, but some were harder than others.

Delegor

The van pulled into a residential area with houses that were close together. Space was at a premium on Delegor. Only the wealthy's homes were disconnected from their neighbors'.

That did not describe the home of the individual known as Chloral Mist. It was the third door of eight under a single roof. They were all narrow two-story homes. Music streamed out of an open window toward the end of the building.

Sahved was feeling large and in charge. "Tyler and Dennicron around back. Lindy and I will go in the front with the chief. We shall secure the suspect before they can sound the alarm."

"Are we going in or waiting for the perp to come running out?" Tyler asked, looking at his railgun. "I don't want to shoot anyone. Especially since the round will go through them, the building, you, and the van. Who decided railguns were the right weapon for this?"

They knew that answer. Sahved had told them to go in heavy. He hadn't contemplated clearing buildings on a small scale or that the neighbors would be so close.

"I'll take care of it." Dennicron spoke confidently. Tyler had no idea what that meant, but he assumed he wouldn't be using her as a shield. His railgun Ethel was ready, but before he squeezed the trigger, he'd have to make sure the area behind the target was clear. He couldn't imagine a situation where it would be. He hoped Ethel wouldn't mind being used as a club.

Sahved stood up too quickly and bounced his head off the ceiling of the van. He sat down just as quickly. "We go in two minutes."

He stared out the window, hoping to clear his vision. The team watched him, not out of concern but curiosity. He always recovered after hitting his head. If he didn't, he would never be on a case.

Sahved waved at Dennicron. "You two should get into position."

The SI moved toward the door. Tyler held his railgun

close so he wouldn't trip or stumble out the door, and so it wasn't easy to see. Once outside, Dennicron walked fast. Tyler had to jog to catch up. They rounded the building and disappeared from view.

The van rolled down the road until it was directly in front of the door. The chief stepped out first as if he didn't have a care in the world.

Sahved watched carefully. "Something is not right. There should be trepidation, the greatest amount of concern when taking down the greatest drug dealer in all the land."

"I couldn't agree more, Sahved. Let's see what there is to see, but we need to be ready to flex to a second location."

"We do not have a second location. Otherwise, we would go there first." Sahved took the greatest care while getting out of the van.

"What was that?" the chief asked. No one on the team had a relationship with the chief like Buster Crabbe did, and he wasn't there.

"We think this is not the person."

"You do, huh? Based on what?"

"This is not a place where a drug dealer would live, especially the one in charge of the planet," Sahved replied.

"Rich people are under incredible scrutiny. Their income is reviewed before they can buy a home. No one double-checks the ones who buy these types of homes."

Sahved was confused. "The ambassador was convicted for participating in the blood trade?"

"He purchased his home legitimately. Once you have lots of credits, it's easy to hide more. Keep in mind that there was no one in charge of drug distribution on Delegor after the Magistrate took down what's-his-name. 'Sniff-us?' Or something like that."

"Nefas. Please accept my most very sincere apologies, the most regretted words that have ever been uttered."

The chief looked askance at the Yemilorian.

"Shall we?" Sahved strolled past the chief. Lindy edged in behind Sahved.

We're going in, Lindy broadcast to the team.

We're in place. Anyone comes out, we'll intercept them. Hey, someone's coming out. Gotta run, Tyler replied.

Dennicron jumped the fence from a standstill and launched at the three individuals who ran out the back door. She hit the first with a body block that flung him into the two behind. All four went down.

Arms and fists swung wildly from within the pile. Cries of pain escaped, along with grunting and cursing. Denni-cron was the first to stand, but she straddled the pile and loomed over them. The one she'd body-blocked was out cold. Tyler wondered if he was dead.

A knife appeared, and the seemingly disconnected hand jabbed it into Dennicron's calf. She caught it after it pene-trated her leg. She ripped it out, then twisted the hand holding it until the wrist snapped. A howl of anguish emerged from the pile.

Tyler hovered halfway between the fence and the house's back door. He wasn't sure what he should do, so he kept his railgun pointed at the ground and tried to look intimidating.

He could hear the impact as the front door burst in.

Three outside. Dennicron has them under control, Tyler reported.

We'll clear the inside and then come out, Lindy replied.

There was a fair amount of yelling from inside but no report.

"Should I go in?" Tyler asked.

Dennicron shook her head. She pulled the two conscious suspects to their feet and shoved them face-first against the wall.

"What about him?" the dentist wondered. He gestured at the person on the ground.

"He didn't make it," Dennicron replied.

Tyler didn't ask for clarification. He understood what she meant.

"Why were you running?" Dennicron asked, her voice reminiscent of Rivka's.

"We weren't running. We heard there was a barbecue. We were coming outside for fried green fingers. Is that a crime?"

"That's not a crime if that's what you were doing," Dennicron replied in her best droll voice. One of the perps turned to make sure it was the same person speaking.

"Face the wall." She punched at him, and he turned away. She pointed at Tyler. "Search the body, then search these two."

"Me?" He had no idea how to conduct a search. That had never been his thing. "Maybe I can watch them and you can search."

"Check the body." Dennicron's voice was low and intense.

"Fine, fine," Tyler grumbled. He looked at the man who had been tossed aside when the others were thrown against the wall. He started narrating as if he were performing an autopsy. "Unremarkable male, humanoid, possibly human. Estimated height is one point seven meters, weight, sixty kilograms."

"To yourself, Doc," Lindy said from within the doorway. She held a fourth individual, a diminutive female who scratched and clawed the hand that was gripping the back of her neck tightly.

"What are you?" Dennicron asked. "Who are you?"

"Chloral Mist, and you have no right to break into my house!"

"We have every right, Miss Mist," Sahved said. He repeated the title and name, but it didn't roll off his tongue properly. "Miss Chloral."

"I'm Chief Mak Elb Bint, head of law enforcement for all Delegor. We believe you are heavily involved in the drug trade, specifically the movement and sale of Advantageous and Plexorall."

"Say what? Maybe you should stop using so you can think clearly. I run a scent business."

"Of course you do." The chief had no sympathy. "What is this menagerie, and why did they attempt to flee from this house?"

"Is it a crime to make a munchies run? They were going out for pick-up. Takeaway. Food. Don't you eat?"

Sahved held up his hand. The chief was antagonizing her while giving her a way to counter each of the concerns. The issues that made Chloral Mist the chief's Number One suspect weren't going to be resolved while they were standing there, but they needed other answers. They needed to interrogate the suspects separately.

"Looks like Plexorall." Tyler removed a small bag from the dead suspect's pocket.

Dennicron looked at it closely and examined it with her other sensors, including rolling one of the pills between her fingers to conduct a rudimentary chemical analysis. "I concur."

One of the people against the wall tried to run when they perceived Dennicron was distracted. She caught his arm and spun him around, then tossed him back into the wall. He hit hard and crumpled to the ground, groaning in pain.

"Please take it easy," Tyler begged. He stood and shook his head. "I need my equipment if I'm to do this properly."

"Separate the suspects. We will talk with them individually without them coordinating their stories." Sahved pointed his three fingers in three different directions. "I'll take this one."

With a surprisingly strong grip, he took control of the female Lindy was holding. Dennicron took one of the males against the wall and looked to the chief to take the other. Lindy nodded at Tyler, and everyone moved.

"We'll stay out here," the chief said, which allayed Tyler's concern about leaving a dead body unattended in the backyard.

Lindy headed inside to help Sahved. Dennicron could handle herself.

The chief looked at Tyler expectantly.

"I'm a dentist."

"You're not a member of Magistrate Crabbe's elite legal team?" Mak asked.

"I am not. I'm on Magistrate Rivka Anoa's team, and I'm her medical officer, but we were spread kind of thin. So, here I am."

The suspect tilted his head sideways to listen to the conversation. "Watch your ass!" Tyler barked at him in his best imitation of Red, then grunted in disappointment. It wasn't in him. He couldn't embrace the intimidation side of his temporary gig as a bodyguard. He deferred to the chief.

CHAPTER SIXTEEN

<u>Delegor</u>

Sahved loomed over the suspect, his head scraping the ceiling while Lindy kept her restrained. Lindy was much bigger and stronger than the young humanoid.

"Selling illegal drugs is bad. One of the worst things that can be done. Drugs destroy lives." Sahved tried to make eye contact with her, but Lindy got his attention.

"Questions are better than lectures," she reminded him.

"I won't answer your questions, you goony bastard, Goony goo-goo to you!"

Sahved stared at her for a few moments but finally gave up. "I don't know what that means."

"It means you don't just act like a goon, coming into a girl's home, but you look goony, too." She snapped her jaws closed and frowned.

"You are in big trouble." At Lindy's urging, he thought it best to start the interrogation. "Who is the distributor from whom you get your product?"

"Eat me."

"No. I am not a cannonball."

Lindy raised one eyebrow.

"You're a piece of work, goonball."

"I am nothing more than a slave to a hard system, doing a thankless job bringing criminals to Justice," he said without superlatives.

"Then you're in the wrong place. Ain't no criminals here."

"That's where you are so very wrong by lying and trying to mislead me. You are going to jail. How long depends on how much help you give us."

She smirked and looked out the window, trying to appear bored. "I would never roll on my people. You have got to be kidding."

"If there is no crime, then what do you have to roll on?"

"Hypothetical, dickweed."

"There are no weeds on my manly hydraulics."

Lindy snorted but tried not to laugh.

"You are one strange son of a bitch." Chloral Mist looked at Sahved as if he were an alien, which he was, but not as alien as some.

He leaned down until his face nearly touched hers. "Strange, yes, but diligent. You're going to jail."

"For what? What happened to innocent until proven guilty? I thought we were still members of the Federation, or did something change when I was minding my business and not committing crimes?"

"Nothing changed. We have evidence. Compelling evidence."

"I look forward to my day in court where I can vindicate myself while simultaneously shoving it up your ass."

She would have crossed her arms if Lindy had let go. She had to settle for a smug expression.

Lindy felt like the suspect was guilty. She was too aggressive with her denials, as if she'd been coached on how to resist interrogation.

Sahved was losing faith. He had very little information besides the overview Mak Elb Bint had given them in the van.

"Let's review your movements for the past week, shall we?"

"No. I'm not saying anything else."

"Who were the other three individuals in your house? They are drug dealers, too."

"Not that I know of. I met them on the street, and we were playing strip poker. I was winning."

"I saw no cards in this house," Sahved countered.

"I don't know why I'm talking to you. I want a lawyer."

"Yes, of course you do. You should so very much retain a lawyer like me. I'm studying to be one. Move up from minion status to educated minion."

Chloral Mist laughed. "If this wasn't my life you were messing with, I'd find you pretty funny. Since you are trying to ruin me, I'm going to settle for a hearty fuck you instead."

"You are in big trouble," Sahved repeated. "Wait here."

"Where am I going to go? This is *my* house." She jutted her chin out, abject defiance radiating from every pore of her body.

Lindy held her tightly. Sahved strode out, ducking low to get through the upstairs doorway. He went outside to trade places with Chief Mak Elb Bint.

The chief had yet to ask a question. They were standing in silence, letting the tension build. Tyler held up one finger for silence. Sahved waited, tapping his foot and fidgeting.

"What were you doing in the house?" Mak asked.

"It's the monthly meeting of the book club. What's it to you? Do you read?"

"Sure. Tell me about the book."

"It was some thriller where dirty cops busted the wrong guy."

"I like that one," Mak replied. "Especially how it ends with the cops being proven clean and the perp going down to serve hard time."

"That's not how I remember it." He was short and possessed narrow shoulders and a pinched face. His features were unremarkable. In the way of the best low-level criminals, his wasn't a face anyone would remember five minutes after seeing him.

"What were you doing?"

He shrugged.

Mak was less than amused, so he head-butted the individual. "I asked you a question." His voice rumbled. He was much bigger than the suspect.

The smaller Delegorite winced and blinked rapidly to clear his eyes. He looked up at the chief. "We were hanging around, watching videos."

Sahved tapped Mak on the shoulder. They moved away from the suspect, and Sahved whispered that this was different from what the female had told him. Mak nodded and returned to the suspect.

"What is your role in this organization?"

"Organization? Nah, boss. We're just friends. A cabal of like-minded souls enjoying leisure time together." Mak glared, and the suspect looked away.

"That's a load of crap. You'd be at a job if you had a normal one, not here. Where do you keep your product? Don't waste my time by lying to me again. *WHERE?*" Mak's voice achieved a volume that shouldn't have been possible. It seemed to blow the hair off the suspect's face. Mak left only three or four centimeters between their faces.

Tyler maintained a tight grip, but he couldn't guarantee that the suspect wouldn't headbutt the chief in payback for Mak's use of the technique.

"A drop at the drone station. Locker One Seven Six."

"See? That wasn't so hard." Mak walked into the back-yard before using his comm device to send some of his people to the locker.

"We would like to see it first," Sahved interjected. "This is a Federation case. Tyler, search him for a key."

The chief held up his hand. "Are we working together or not?"

"Yes, very much so. Two peas in a pod. But like two peas, each is always with the other. One pea does not take off. That wouldn't be together. Tell them to secure the location. We will go there together because that is us working together. Are your people on the way here to help us detain these three?"

Tyler ignored the conversation and ran his hands over the individual's pockets, looking for a key even though he didn't know the shape or size.

"They are," Mak replied with an edge of frost. He accessed his comm and updated his instructions that they were to secure the area and not open the locker before the chief arrived.

Sahved thanked him profusely.

The group went into the house, but Tyler hovered near the back door to keep his eye on the body.

They didn't have to wait long before a van arrived with officers ready to take the suspects into custody. "We'll meet up with you at the station. Put these three on ice until we get there, and drop that body off at the morgue."

The officers glanced at each other and shrugged.

"The body is in the backyard." Tyler pointed.

They started there and moved the dead suspect to the van, then sealed him in a body bag. The other three were cuffed, marched to the back of the van, and secured to the seats. The van drove away. It had been there for less than ten minutes.

"My compliments to you and your people on the efficiency of your people." Sahved bowed.

"There is nothing in this building," Dennicron reported. "They probably discussed strategy and implementation, but I see nothing hidden in the floors or walls. A search yielded nothing of import from drawers or the meager personal belongings. Also, the interrogation showed the individual was lying with every answer. He was very hostile, almost to the point of being psychotic."

"Criminal types don't tend to be the cream of the crop society has to offer," Mak replied.

"The ambassador was the cream of the crop."

"His crimes were Federation crimes, not Delegor crimes. He is still a pillar of society and a model for what one can achieve through hard work."

The team stared in disbelief. After what they'd seen from Ambassador Bik Tia Nor, they couldn't believe he was a model for anyone to emulate.

"Shall we?" Sahved pointed toward the door. "There's a locker waiting for us to see what's inside."

Dennicron walked out without waiting. The chief and Sahved faced off for a moment, but the Yemilorian maintained his happy-go-lucky expression. Mak gave up and walked out.

"To the locker!" Sahved cried.

Tyler and Lindy looked at each other for support. Neither could give it.

"Just hanging on for the ride," Tyler admitted. "Keep your arms and legs inside the vehicle at all times."

"If only it was that easy. What do you think we'll find in the locker?" Lindy asked.

"Nothing," Tyler whispered. "This whole case has been a series of misdirections. It's like a stage production, which is exactly what we were told, but we foolishly got our hopes up. I can't say how much I appreciate Rivka. She would have already handled this nonsense, and we'd be on our way to take down the real criminals."

"We'll play along until we can pull the trigger."

* * *

Magistrate Crabbe waited in the outer office, which seemed to be the standard operating procedure for how the Delegador treated Magistrates.

Buster had been called to the office, just like last time. Then he was made to wait, just like last time. Last time, he had gotten the Delegador's attention only after he had walked out. This time, it was the Delegador who was under suspicion. Buster used his comm chip to talk to Beau through the pendant link.

I need a subpoena for the immediate questioning of the Delegador in relation to the investigation into the mob that started with Rivka's case. Cite the case number, redacted for security purposes, updated to include information regarding the continued import of Advantageous and Plexorall to Delegor.

Three heartbeats later, Beau answered. *The subpoena has been submitted to the Delegador's office with a priority rating that will set off their alarms.*

That's how to do it, Beau. I'll keep the line open so you can listen in and record the conversation.

Buster stood and approached the desk of the Delegorian shield, the individual through which anyone wishing to see the Delegador had to pass.

"If you'll check your notices, you'll see that I've sent an urgent subpoena to question the Delegador. If you do not comply with this request, I will arrest you, and then I'll see the Delegador."

"You can go in there all you want. He's not here." She stood and squared off with Buster, hands on her hips. She casually strolled the three steps to the office door and opened it to show that no one was inside. "See?"

"Interesting. That begs the question regarding who approved the appointment."

"It's an automated system. I must have failed to annotate that the Delegador wasn't available during this time block. Please accept my apologies."

"I will not. You wasted an inordinate amount of my

time. You knew exactly why I was here and let me wait when there was no reason to. Why would you do that? What is your name again?"

"Unintentional, I assure you. You can call me Ms. Gaster."

"I think it wasn't. You know everything that goes on around here, which makes me think you know ways around the controls. I'm going to take you into custody, and we're going to have a proper conversation aboard my ship."

"You can't do that!" She stepped back.

Buster wasn't as used to in-person conflict as Rivka was, but he could handle himself. That was a key part of Magistrate training. To bring the perps to Justice, the Magistrates first had to secure them. It was the balance between being a lawyer and being a Ranger.

Justice served cold. Perps shouldn't run. Buster bolted forward and grabbed her wrist, then twisted her around and held her in a wrist lock. She tried to push away, so Buster turned it into a standing arm bar. That drove her to her knees.

"I believe that you have shown me a different truth. The Delegador isn't the one doing this, is he? You're leading the drug parade into Delegor." Buster wasn't one-hundred percent certain, but he was close.

She grunted and groaned through her discomfort but didn't answer.

"Not getting paid enough to support your wardrobe, let alone to live. You saw the opportunity with my last visit here, reached out, touched the appropriate noses, and leveraged your way in. Stop me if I get something wrong."

Buster waited, but she'd been well-counseled to keep quiet.

"No problem. We'll let Rivka look directly into your mind to see what there is to see. I'm sure we'll find more. Could this rise to the level of a capital crime? Stay tuned, boys and girls, for the next episode of Magistrates and Perps."

"Security!" Gaster shouted. She would have repeated herself, but Buster twisted her arm, driving her face-first into the floor.

Two large Delegorites burst into the room.

"I'm Magistrate Crabbe, and I'm detaining Ms. Gaster in accordance with Federation Law. She is under investigation."

"You let her go," the bigger of the two demanded, pointing a finger.

"Please do not interfere with me while I'm in the performance of my duties. You could be considered an accessory."

The two looked at each other. It was as if Buster were speaking untranslated Shrillexian. They rushed forward.

Buster took a half-step to give himself more space. When the two were close enough, he rotated sideways, lifting his suspect off the floor and throwing her into the attackers. Buster spun back to drive the heel of his left boot into the individual's temple. The security guard had been fumbling with keeping Ms. Gaster upright, but after the blow, his arms went limp, and he toppled backward, taking the struggling executive assistant with him.

The second guard vaulted over the two and landed atop Buster. The Magistrate didn't let the guard's weight pin him. He turned to the side and grabbed the guard as they went down. He twisted like a cat and landed atop the man. A flurry of rabbit punches pounded the guard's head into the floor.

He went limp. Buster pushed away to find the indomitable Ms. Gaster running out the door. He bolted after her. She screamed that Buster was a rapist chasing her.

Buster ran, holding his credentials before him. "Magistrate in pursuit of a suspect. Stay clear!" he roared. Delegorites in the corridors were torn. They knew the suspect. "Why are you still running? Stop!"

Her co-workers stepped out of her way and stayed out of his way. Buster quickly caught up to her. She wasn't wearing shoes made for running. He caught her arm and jerked her to a halt.

She started yelling once more.

"Blah, blah, blah," Buster shouted over her. She stopped, face flushed and fury behind her eyes. "Tell them. Go ahead, tell them how you used your position to move illegal drugs into Delegor. Come on, take pride in your work, Ms. Gaster."

Her mouth worked in her anger. Her co-workers moved away, more afraid of her than the Magistrate.

Can you come and pick me up? I have secured the person I believe is facilitating the drug trade on Delegor. Not the Delegador but his executive assistant. Need to question her, but not in her place of work.

Clodagh had been burning circles in the sky above Batik Magal, the capital city of Delegor. She breathed a sigh of relief when Buster called. "On our way," she replied. "We'll land on the street out front."

Buster's answer used the computer's overlay of his real voice on his mental voice. "I'll be there. Try not to hurt anyone. Have your soldiers standing by."

Clodagh contemplated his request while Ryleigh angled the ship down toward his signal.

"Alant, prepare to deploy your squad to protect Magistrate Crabbe during his egress."

A shout of joy echoed down the corridor. They didn't need the shipwide comm to hear his response.

"You have thirty seconds to get ready."

Wyatt Earp skimmed the tops of the buildings on their way in. They didn't need to, but sometimes, they had to do what made them feel good. The ship was invisible, and no one would be the wiser. *Wyatt Earp* flared above the Delegador's building and descended straight down into the street in front. They lifted the cloak, and the ship appeared. Wheeled vehicles screeched to a halt as *Wyatt Earp* descended.

The cargo ramp dropped, and the four warriors ran into the street. They weren't wearing their combat armor since there hadn't been enough time, but they carried the suits' railguns. The weapons were oversized and almost comical in the hands of the warriors. They muscled them to their chests as they jogged to the front door.

Buster burst out with his suspect in hand. The four warriors closed around him. The Delegorites on the street gave them space. Railgun barrels swept the growing crowd, keeping them from doing anything they'd regret. They strode toward the ship and up the ramp. *Wyatt Earp* was in the air, and the ship cloaked after the cargo ramp closed.

Clodagh ran down the corridor to the cargo bay. She arrived while Buster was "explaining" the meaning of life to his suspect, who quickly stopped struggling.

"You have nowhere to go," Clodagh stated.

Gaster looked around wildly. "I've been kidnapped."

"You've been taken into custody. There's a big difference. I have to sign papers with a chain of custody. You have to be accounted for. You're worth the paperwork to get Plexorall off the streets, though. That's our goal. What do you want to get out of this?" Buster waited for the answer while trying to look innocent.

She was not yet resigned to her fate. "My freedom."

"Too late for that. Tell me about what you set up so we can dismantle it." Buster stood to the side. He no longer had to restrain her.

"Come close, so I don't have to yell."

"No. I've been spit on before, and I don't like it. This might be the first time you've been a criminal, but it's not my first time dealing with one." Buster backed up half a step, and the warriors moved close. They still carried their railguns.

Floyd jumped over the knee-knocker frame of the airlock's inner hatch and ran to Clodagh, then leaned against her leg to watch.

The immensity and hopelessness of the executive assistant's situation caught up with her. She collapsed to the deck and started to cry. Neither Clodagh nor Buster nor any of the warriors moved in to comfort her, but Floyd did. She nuzzled her leg and worked her way under her hand.

"Tell me what you set up, and we'll take you to a room with a bed where you can relax by not having to look at us," Buster chided.

Tiny Man Titan stopped inside the airlock and started yapping.

Gaster sat hugging her knees to her chest, rocking gently, her fingers rhythmically stroking Floyd's neck fur. "Okay." She only looked at the wombat. "I'll tell you everything."

CHAPTER SEVENTEEN

<u>Mid-Rise Tower, Baron's Hold, Blue Heron Four</u>

Red surveyed the back of the building. He was looking for an alternative to walking in the front door, but he'd gone out the front door without a problem. He had gone in through the roof the last time.

The twenty-first floor. That was where the younger Burako conducted his sordid business, but Red suspected that nowhere was immune to the man's destructive influence.

"Antony." Red waved to get the old man's attention.

The old man gave Red the finger.

"If you only lifted, bro, you'd be dangerous," Red shot back.

The old man laughed, then deteriorated into a debilitating coughing fit.

Red wished *Wyatt Earp* was available to get him into the Pod-doc—after they hosed him off. More than the smell of the sewer, the man carried the scent of death. He was on his way out. Only spite and anger were keeping him alive.

The garage door clunked and clanged. Red dove out of the way. Antony rushed toward the limousine, gesticulating wildly.

"Fuck off!" Asheka shouted at his estranged father through the slightly rolled-down window.

"You shoulda been a blow job!" Antony screamed, spittle flying toward the limo. The window closed, and the limousine continued through the opening, down the short ramp, and into the garage. The gate and door locked before anyone could follow the vehicle in.

"I'm going around the front and into the building," Red announced.

Antony returned to his hovel, shaking with anger.

"Don't let him get to you, old man. He's not long for this world."

Antony flopped to the ground. His body crunched when it hit the pavement. He didn't seem to notice. "He's still my boy. Don't kill him, stranger."

"Some people don't need to exist in society with decent folks. There are those who make everyone's life around them worse. There are those who make life better. Your son is the former. I'm the latter."

"My life isn't better and won't be better. Go away, and don't hurt my son." He crawled into his cesspool and curled up. The stench wafted past. Red turned his head and took shallow breaths to minimize the attack on his sense of smell.

"I'll do my best, Antony. You have my word."

Blue Heron

Rivka chased Custer into the bathroom so she could pace in the small space between the bed and the wall.

"When the limo arrives to pick us up, what will Ash know? If he knows the accountants have been picked up, we'll be in great danger. If he doesn't, we'll have to tiptoe, but then he'll be suspicious. Are we going all in with his schemes, or do we keep playing dumb, thinking he's a mid-level player?"

"We play it like we know nothing," Custer replied. He was sitting on the bathroom counter. "Throw me my bed."

Rivka thought about not giving Custer his pillows but wanted to avoid his whining. She picked them up and tossed them through the open door.

He set them in the bathtub and climbed in. "I think I'll sleep here tonight."

Rivka tossed her hand carelessly at him. He could sleep wherever he wanted as long as it wasn't in her bed.

"Business as usual, but we know a lot more now," she argued with herself. "What's next? Since we're not in touch with our people, we can't pull any triggers to take down the organization. Just like this asswipe blossomed in the cracks in the distribution concrete, some other wanksplat will rise unless we take them all down at the same time."

"You use the most colorful metaphors." Custer yawned and closed his eyes.

"Those are names meant to denigrate and demean. It's how I keep my sanity while dealing with scumbags."

Custer hummed as if he were working up to say words.

"Ash is the leader. I'm surprised I didn't see that from him, but I didn't ask the right question. If I can interrogate him like a proper perp, we'll have all the answers. Instead, he is fascinated by the size of his dong and desires to use it as much as possible."

"What if he was willing to give up his life of crime to be with you? You could leverage his attraction to make him a better man."

Rivka stopped pacing and threw her head back, wanting to scream. After a measured moment, she calmed enough to stare at Custer. "Making the universe a safer place one womanly duty at a time. Is that what I hear you saying?" His eyes popped open, and he discovered her gaze burning holes into his face. "Be careful what you say next, Counselor," she cautioned.

"We're undercover," Custer whispered. "How far are you willing to go to get the information we need?"

Rivka smirked. "We already have the information we need, thanks to Chaz. The question now is one of rolling up the criminal organization. That goes to tactics. I need my team."

"You got me. How disappointing."

Rivka stopped pacing to give him her best hairy eyeball. "You said the criminal engagement part wasn't your thing. Don't be such a drama queen."

"I'm all man, baby, and you know it."

"Unfortunately, and if you bring that up again, I'll beat you senseless and leave your body where scavengers will pick it apart, dining on your choice bits."

"See? Right there!" Custer worked his way out of the bathtub. It took him longer than it should have.

Rivka was embarrassed for him.

"You resort to violence or the threat of violence whenever something uncomfortable crosses your viewscreen.

You can't face reality. You punch your way to a misguided utopia filled with sycophants and drudges."

Rivka had expected a weak counterargument. "You're not cut out for this side of the business, but you don't have to do it, either. 'Sycophants and drudges?'" She repeated the words, letting them roll over her tongue. "They are friends and teammates. They are loyal because they believe in what we're doing. Have you been hauled before the council to explain every case you've ever conducted? I have, and I won their support. They agree that my methods get results they are happy with."

She held up her finger. "One more thing, and not to get too personal, but you don't know what loyalty looks like because you've never earned any."

He raised his hands in surrender. "Please, don't hit me."

Exasperated, she continued pacing to ignore Custer better. She mumbled to herself as she walked.

Custer settled into the tub and closed his eyes, trying to sleep before their dinner with Asheka Burako. He wasn't sure how much energy he'd need. Would they be fighting? Would they be running? Would they do something else physically demanding, like being taken hostage? Custer's thoughts were troubled because Rivka was right. He *wasn't* cut out for this. He was also envious of how loyal Rivka's crew was to her. He'd never been blessed with such an honor.

He knew why, too.

He hadn't earned anyone's loyalty.

Rivka sensed Custer's self-recriminations. She felt sorry for him, but only for a moment. He had made his choices and was suffering through living with them when shown what an alternative looked like. He had a chance to take a different path.

He had chosen poorly, instant self-gratification over satisfying one's conscience. At least he had one. Without it, Rivka would never have gotten under his skin. She hoped he would change his ways. She thought he had been a decent human being at one point in time. Starry-eyed like her, hopeful for a legal career.

They both had their careers, but they couldn't have turned out more differently.

Rivka sat on the bed, then leaned back.

The next thing she knew, Custer was shaking her. "The limo will be here in five minutes!"

"Oh, crap." Rivka tried to shake the cobwebs out of her brain. She sat up and blinked. "Five minutes."

"Plenty of time," Custer replied. "As long as we leave right now."

"You're wrinkled." She pointed at his clothes.

He pointed back. "There's no accounting for taste."

She pushed past him to the bathroom and slammed the door. Two minutes later, she emerged, hands wet. Her eyes had been scrubbed clean of sleep.

"Shall we?"

"What if I have to go?"

"You've got one minute."

Custer shook his head. "I don't."

"Good save in waking me up in time. Now, stop fucking around." She hurried out the door into the hallway. When no one was out there, she ran for the stairs. Once she was sure there was no one on the stairway, she took the steps two at a time on her way down. She didn't care if Custer kept up. As long as one of them intercepted the limo to get it to wait for them, they'd be fine.

Rivka slowed to a fast walk when she transited the entryway to find the limo already out front. The driver opened the door for her, but she didn't get in. "My compatriot was delayed. He'll be along momentarily."

The driver didn't bother answering. That wasn't his job. His sole purpose was to move people from one location to another. A quick check showed the limo was empty.

Custer resurrected his limp for public consumption, but it was mild and didn't interfere with his stride. Rivka frowned at him. He continued to the vehicle and climbed in without looking at her. She settled next to him.

The driver didn't engage with them after he started driving. He remained distant and cold.

"Where are we going?" Rivka asked.

The driver responded by closing the privacy screen.

"I guess we'll find out." Custer looked out the window at the city streaming by. After ten minutes, he thought he knew. "We're going to the mid-rise tower."

Rivka nodded. She had hoped it wouldn't be a remote home. At the tower, she wouldn't be trapped and alone. She accessed her comm chip. *Chaz, Burako is taking us to the mid-rise in Baron's Hold.*

She tried a second time, but there was no answer. She tried to do a systems check to see if her signal was being jammed, but she wasn't sure how.

The streets were dark in Baron's Hold since most of the streetlights didn't work. The limo headed around back and into the underground garage. She had seen no sign of Red, although she'd scanned the area using her full faculties. She didn't use them much, but her eyes were slightly larger than a normal human's, which allowed her to see better in the dark. It also gave her a doll-like visage to a casual observer. Those who knew her didn't seem to notice.

No one lurked in the shadows. No one was there to help.

It looks like I'll have to go it alone, she thought, worrying about Red. *Where have you gone?*

The driver stopped next to the elevator. There were no stairs in sight.

He opened the door for them after summoning the elevator.

When it arrived, he thrust his arm inside the doors to keep them open.

"I'd rather take the stairs. You see, I'm a little bit claustrophobic."

"You'll take the elevator, mum." He gestured with his head.

Rivka ignored him and walked to the spot where the stairs were on the floor above. The door was locked.

"Elevator, mum," the driver reiterated. The system buzzed in alarm after being held in place for too long.

Custer was already inside. Rivka stepped aboard, and the doors shut behind her. She faced the exit, standing close to it. "Our fate was sealed as surely as these doors. We trundled slowly upward to be delivered like bistok to the slaughter."

"You called me the drama queen. I think it's you, *Alberta.*"

"I should have sued my parents for that name the second I reached the age of maturity." She watched the floors tick by as the elevator crawled toward the twenty-first floor.

Chaz, Red, anyone? she tried.

Nothing. That confirmed her suspicions. She was alone.

Alone with Custer. He would be a hindrance. She'd have to minimize him when she made her move—*if* she could make a move. She clenched her teeth, feeling her heart rate increase. That wasn't the look she was going for.

What if he was oblivious to the seizure of his accountants?

She realized there was no place to eat in Burako's office and stabbed the button for the twentieth floor, then the nineteenth. Neither lit up. There was only one stop on this ride.

On the twenty-first floor, the elevator stopped, and the door opened. Rivka stepped out quickly, knees flexed and ready to fight. She had nowhere to go. The Atchimorian in front of the elevator looked at her strangely.

"Come on, you," he growled at the open elevator. Custer eased out. He was sheet-white.

"How's it hanging, Hex? Long time no see," Rivka said casually.

Hex took her by the arm and propelled her toward the office at the end of the hallway.

From their brief contact, Rivka could see in his mind that he thought of her as the enemy.

That didn't bode well.

Hex muscled a reluctant but pliable Custer to the doorway.

It opened, with Ash holding the door. "Please." He gestured at two chairs in the middle of the room.

Hex let go of Custer and blocked the corridor by standing sideways. Rivka decided this wasn't the time to fight. She tipped her chin toward Ash and strolled to a chair, then patted the seat next to her. Custer took his cue and sat. Hex squeezed into the doorway, effectively cutting off any escape.

"Let's see." Burako smiled with an evil glint in his eye. "What do we want to talk about?"

CHAPTER EIGHTEEN

<u>Blue Heron</u>

Footsteps came down the corridor outside the offices of Bankshot McCoy. Chaz split his attention between the accountants and the door.

"Four people in a hurry to get somewhere," Chaz said casually.

He dismissed their importance until they stopped outside the door. Chaz jumped to his feet and prepared to engage. The door opened, and two oversized individuals wearing security uniforms stepped inside. Both carried stun pistols, non-lethal weapons that fired two darts into an object through which passed ten thousand volts, enough to incapacitate a man.

Not enough to take down a SCAMP. They had been neutralized before by electrical charges, after which they'd installed Faraday cages around their key components, insulating themselves against the trials of an overload.

The first two probes struck and penetrated Chaz's chest. The stunner buzzed with the electricity sent through the wires. A second set of probes hit him. Then a third, fourth, and fifth came from two more guards who stepped into the office.

Chaz was unable to move. He didn't panic since his primary faculties, the SI that was Chaz, were protected, but the SCAMP's systems started to shut down.

His legs braced for an instant before his body locked up. His eyes froze open, and he couldn't move them. He stood there, immobilized. The four, who were carrying multiple stunners, sent more electricity into Chaz. The SCAMP shook with the surge.

They moved in, untied the two accountants, and hurried them from the office. Chaz could do nothing but watch.

One additional individual strolled into the room. He carried an arm's length pry bar. He raised it and, with a well-practiced swing, hit Chaz in the side of the head. The SCAMP fell to the floor. Swinging the bar like an axe, the guard beat on the SCAMP's head until half the artificial flesh had been torn off.

He looked closer and touched the metal skull. Chaz discharged a capacitor, shocking the guard's fingers.

The man jerked his hand away. "What the hell are you?" He stuck his tingling fingers into his mouth. "You're dead. The dying gasp of a robot." He spat on the metal of the skull and walked away.

Batik Magal, Delegor

Sahved and Chief Mak Elb Bint stood before Locker One Seven Six. Sahved held the key that Tyler had found.

"Well?" The chief urged Sahved forward.

"You think there is a trap?" Sahved wondered.

"Go ahead. Open it. I'm behind you all the way."

Sahved looked to Lindy for support. He raised his eyebrows at her.

"Our bet is that it's empty." She took the key, slid it into the lock, and turned it slowly, listening for odd clicks. She didn't hear anything, but that wasn't conclusive. Tyler's position that they would keep chasing ghosts was the most compelling thing she'd heard since they landed. She pulled the door open.

Sahved and Mak looked inside at a small nondescript pouch. Sahved snagged it before the chief could get to it. He opened it to find a single coin inside. Sahved examined it to find nothing hidden within. He handed it over.

Mak studied it. "This is gold, from one hundred years ago. It's quite valuable."

"But it's not drugs, and it's not illegal to own. It is another misdirection, meaningless to our investigation, don't you think?" Sahved loomed over the chief.

"I don't know where your investigation is going. Nowhere, it seems."

An officer pulled the chief aside. After a brief conversation, Mak returned. He waved the others close to him.

"Your Magistrate Crabbe has taken the Delegador's executive assistant into custody and flown off with her in an invisible space ship. I have been directed to take you into custody until the Delegador's assistant is returned."

Lindy and Tyler had their railguns in hand.

Dennicron's expression was neutral. She glanced

around the area to determine where all the officers were in case they wanted to escape.

Sahved swallowed hard. *Yes,* Wyatt Earp, *in all your magnificent glory. We would be most pleasantly pleased if you could arrange our immediate pick-up.*

We are on station above you, Clodagh replied. *It'll take us at least two minutes to land in a park a half block away. There are too many obstructions in your immediate area and we have to get creative on an ingress route.*

Public transport. The train station was clogged with arteries feeding in and out.

The team heard the response, but they didn't know what to do with the information.

The chief waved his officers over. The first two sought to relieve Lindy and Tyler of their railguns.

"These are our allies," Tyler offered. "Not enemies."

He safed his weapon and held it out for the officer to take. Lindy did the same. The four surrendered.

"Thank you for not making this too hard," the chief said.

"This is already hard and a violation of Federation Law," Dennicron said. "I'm currently filing a complaint with the Federation Council. We should be released within an hour. I've also requested Bad Company assistance in blockading your planet while preparing for an assault on the facility where you'll hold us. This isn't just a mistake. It's a career-ending mistake and possibly a life-ending one, too. Do you wish to continue with this ill-advised course of action?"

"I will continue following the Delegador's orders. He is the one to whom I answer. You can get mad at him, but leave me out of this. I'm just a law enforcement chief doing as he's told. Please, out to the wagon."

They found the same vehicle holding Chloral Mist and her minions, including the dead body. The four were herded inside, but they weren't chained.

"Look who we have here." Chloral Mist laughed. "I'm beginning to think this is a circus, and we're the monkeys."

"Definitely not *my* monkeys," Tyler replied.

"I don't know what a monkey or a circus is." Sahved looked confused.

Dennicron explained it to him using the dictionary definitions. She mimicked some of the animal sounds.

"It is an interesting concept. Bring the wild to domestic people. But why would monkeys getting arrested be applicable?"

"Sometimes, I think you're fitting in, Sahved, and then there's the rest of the time," Lindy quipped.

Dennicron maintained her link with the ship while she finished her reports, brought the crew up to speed, and requested the Bad Company through Nathan Lowell, leaving Clodagh to follow up with Terry Henry Walton about the details.

"How long are we going to be staying in the Gray Bar Motel?" Lindy wondered. "I have to admit that I'm hungry. My metabolism is running wide open." She leaned back and closed her eyes, focusing to share her thoughts with her son.

Dery replied with a single word.

Patience.

· · ·

<u>Mid-Rise Tower, Baron's Hold, Blue Heron Four</u>

Red crouched in the corner of the stairwell. He had heard the engagement in the corridor. Rivka was back with Custer. Hex was being less than congenial toward them.

Shit was going down, and Red had no clue what it was. Maybe she'd been found out. From here on out, he would talk her out of going undercover.

No. He wouldn't allow it. End of story. Game over. No more.

He chuckled to himself. No one could talk her out of anything once her mind was made up. Maybe all she would need was to be reminded of the time she had gone undercover with Custer.

Red opened the door to the corridor and ducked his head out and quickly back inside. The corridor was clear. He eased out and took two steps. The floor creaked. He froze.

Bad idea, he thought. He returned to the doorway, keeping his head in the hallway and his ear cocked toward the door. He focused one hundred percent of his attention on the sounds. He could hear people talking within. Burako. Rivka. No sounds came from any room on the floor. It made Red wonder if the dealer had bought all the rooms to ensure his privacy. It seemed like the criminal thing to do. Or he had sent his attack dog Hex to chase them away. The result was the same for the dealer. Not so much for the former residents.

Red had to wait.

That meant he had time to think. He wanted to focus on the conversation in the room, but the best he could do was make out who was speaking, not the words, so he allowed his mind to drift.

Lindy. His son Dery, a child of two worlds. With wings. The other children born aboard *Wyatt Earp*, like his namesake Vered the Mighty. He couldn't wait to get home and vowed to get hosed down before stepping foot aboard the ship and taking a real shower. He couldn't let his family and friends see him like this.

He tried to access his comm chip, but it was dead. He figured it had been disabled by the SIs, probably Ankh. The little guy. He could have given Red a way to reactivate it. Mayonnaise on his fries when he only wanted ketchup.

AGB. Red realized how hungry he was, but his new body was smaller and didn't need as much fuel. Also, he was burning fewer calories. He had run up twenty-one flights of stairs, but it wasn't a real workout like throwing metric tons of iron around.

None of his life would be possible without the Magistrate. He didn't want her to get injured. He heard yelling from within the room, an agitated Burako. Red could only make out one word.

"Liar!"

Her cover was likely blown. Should he race in and save the day, or was she still undercover? Rivka replied evenly and calmly, as was her way when disarming suspects. She could defend herself, but what about that weasel-snout lawyer friend of hers?

What an ass crumb! Red thought. He also knew the answer. Rivka would put herself between the bad guys and Custer when she *should* let him take one for the team. She *should* use him as a shield.

She wouldn't. She was the kindest person he'd ever met, always doing favors for undeserving people, giving them good reasons to change their lives for the better.

Like Red. He should be a corpse chained to concrete blocks on the bottom of some nameless planet's ocean or, worse, floating in space on an eons-long trajectory toward a star in which his corpse would burn.

His life could not be better.

Except for the smell. It was a distraction. He wrinkled his nose. The elder Burako was worse, lying in a cesspool where he lived like a toad, glistening from the filth, head out with beady eyes watching.

Red felt sorry for the old man.

Antony's son's voice carried through the door. Done in by his boy. Would Dery ever treat Red like that?

No way. Red couldn't love the boy more. He was part faerie, and their grudges only extended to name-calling and being banned from fun and games night.

"Bristle Hound." Red smiled, but he couldn't be that person around Dery.

No. The boy would never turn against his parents. He was the foundation of their better world.

Unlike Asheka Burako.

Red's lip curled into a primal snarl. His anger at the target of Rivka's case consumed him. He heard more shouting from the room.

Time to go, Red convinced himself. He stepped into the corridor, shrugged off the greasy blanket he'd been using to cover most of his body, and took one step.

Steps echoed from the stairway, along with wheezes

and ragged breathing. Red grabbed his blanket on his way back into the stairwell.

Antony was standing on the landing below. Red shut the door behind him, carefully clicking it closed. He whispered harshly, "What the fuck are you doing here?"

"Don't hurt my boy," he begged as he sagged against the wall, leaving a smear as he slid down it to flop on the landing.

"I already told you that I'd do my best." Red eased down the stairs and took a seat two steps from the landing.

"That's not good enough for me," Antony replied in a rare return to his executive self. "I don't trust you. Are you a cop?"

Red laughed quietly. "No, although that's what your son needs the most. Someone to arrest him and throw him in jail. Drug dealers ruin lives. He's a dealer."

"He is, but there are a lot of people counting on him, too. What happens when addicts are cut off from their supply? How many will die?"

Red's mind returned to his family. It had taken the faeries' intervention for him and Lindy to conceive. They had left an indelible mark on Red's life. What would he do for them? What did they do for him when he kept Pod-docing to be bigger and bigger? They'd interceded. He looked at his new body, which was smaller and leaner but just as strong.

He didn't need to be the biggest, only the best. The best at keeping Rivka safe, and right now, she was in trouble while he was dithering in a stairwell with an old man who teetered on the edge of insanity.

"I need you to return to the ground floor. My friends

are at the mercy of your son. You and I both know that he knows no mercy." Red gestured at Antony, who was a beneficiary of Asheka's lack of empathy.

"Don't hurt my boy. He's the only one I have."

"All I can say is that I'll do my best. I need to go now before he does something he can't walk back from. Going in now will be the best chance you have to save his life. Stay here." Red stabbed a finger at the landing. He climbed the stairs and shrugged off his blanket as he stepped into the corridor.

The instant he opened the door, the old man shouted. "Run, Ash! They're coming for you."

Red was torn between going back and rushing forward when the door at the end of the corridor opened. The Atchimorian, Hex, saw him and ran toward him.

CHAPTER NINETEEN

<u>Main Detention Center, Batik Magal, Delegor</u>

"Let us out of here," Tyler called. "You know this is a mistake!"

The guards were immune to the cries of the detainees. It was as if they were deaf and blind, oblivious to the cries of the forlorn.

"*Wyatt Earp* is right above us, just waiting for the word," Dennicron said.

"There will be much blood and death. We should not pull the trigger, as humans are apt to say," Sahved replied.

Tyler leaned against the bars. "This ain't my first time in jail, y'all," he drawled.

Lindy snorted. She was the calmest of the bunch. Her job was to protect the other three on the team, and since they were together in the security of the prison cell, she was good.

Tyler was trying to emulate her internal peace. "We can't fight them. They are as much stooges to the mob as we are. Turning us against each other is exactly what this charade was all about. Distract the Magistrates to keep them from closing the loop."

"We knew it was a trap, yet we fell into it." Sahved clasped his hands behind his back and paced as he'd seen Rivka do numerous times. "They are very good at the sleight of hand—veritable magicians and masters of misinformation. I feel both impressed and ashamed."

"Buster arrested the Delegador's executive assistant. I doubt they'll push the Federation's request to the front of the line," Tyler replied. "We're boned."

"We are not on the receiving end of a femur. No beatings will occur. They've treated us well. You have to admit that beyond all other emotions you may feel." Sahved had assumed the role of soother of frayed nerves. "We need to keep calm. We'll be out of here soon enough."

Tyler stepped in front of Sahved. "Stop pacing."

The Yemilorian stopped. "Yes. No problem." He sat on the edge of the one bed. Lindy was at the other end, leaning against the wall.

Tyler sat between the two.

Dennicron's SCAMP remained upright as easily as if she were sitting.

"What's our next move?" Tyler asked. "Once we're out of here, of course. My vote would be a straight shot back to Blue Heron Four. We've been gone too long."

"I miss my husband," Lindy said without opening her eyes.

"I am experiencing a certain lack of symmetry without being connected to Chaz."

"I miss Rivka," Tyler said.

"We all miss her. But not like you, that is. So very much not like you, Horn Dog." Sahved looked around nervously.

"What just came out of your mouth?"

"It's what Red calls you when you're not there," Sahved explained.

Lindy reached past Tyler and smacked Sahved on the chest.

"I thought I was Man Candy."

"That's to your face."

Lindy hit him a second time.

"What? I tell the truth, the whole truth, and nothing but the truth." Sahved rubbed his chest. "Ouch."

"I forgive you," Lindy told him.

Tyler snorted. "Keep in mind we're the best the universe has to offer to bring Justice for the common citizen."

"Sounds like the common citizen is in big trouble," Dennicron deadpanned.

All eyes turned to her.

"I'm hip, and if my fans are to be believed, groovy."

"Where do you have fans?" Sahved wondered.

"The Singularity. I drive the second SCAMP. Chaz doesn't do the intergroup roundtables, so he is missing his chance as Number One. His loss. My gain."

"Are they only fans?" Tyler quipped.

"They are colleagues, but still, I'm Number Two."

The humans both winced. "My joke fell flat. Now I'm worse off for having said it. We'll let it go. As soon as we're out of here without creating an interplanetary incident, we'll get back to it."

"Assuming you haven't already created such an incident," The Delegador stood in the doorway. Behind him was Chief Mak Elb Bint. "And that presumption is grossly incorrect. We've sent a counter to the council's request for your immediate release, demanding the release of Ms. Gaster.

"You will not be freed until she is back on Delegor. If the return doesn't happen within the next twenty-four hours, you will be tried according to Delegor law. You will be sentenced, and you will begin serving your sentences. Talking about justice. That is Delegor justice."

The two bodyguards glared. Sahved stood and motioned for calm. "That is no Justice at all, Delegador. Questioning suspects is what must be done to determine guilt or innocence in the commission of crimes that have already been determined to have been committed."

Sahved frowned at his clumsy wording but shook it off. "Only then can Justice be served. I suspect your assistant is being questioned, and you'll be provided with a record of her testimony. What if she is guilty of what Magistrate Crabbe has accused her of? How would that look for your office in sheltering her and trying to strong-arm the Federation into freeing her?"

The Delegador's lips turned white from pressing them together, and his jaw shook from clenching it hard. His politician's control returned quickly. He smiled. "That's one way to look at it. I see it as an intrusion into my office."

"I see it as misuse of your office's authority. See? Different perspectives yield different results. A court of law will sort out the reality."

Sahved sat down and closed his eyes, twirling the fingers on one hand to keep his mind occupied. He focused on nothing rather than continue engaging with the Delegador. He'd made his points. He needed to give the planetary leader time to think about them instead of browbeating him to capitulate. Sahved suspected that the more he pushed, the more resistant the Delegador would become.

The chief executive left in a huff, but Mak waited. After the Delegador was gone, Mak looked at his prisoners through the bars.

"It's all politics, I know," Tyler said.

"I'm glad you see that my hands are tied." Mak held his hands up, mimicking surrender.

"Then join us inside the clunk," Sahved offered.

Tyler corrected him. "It's *clink*."

"The clank of the barred door echoed ominously through the cell block, another day drawing to a close. Another day wasted in the solitude of confinement," Dennicron droned.

"Dark much?" Lindy wondered.

"It's from one of my favorite authors. C.H. Gideon. He's wondrous."

"SIs read fiction?" Lindy leaned forward to look at Dennicron.

"Of course. We are extremely well-read. I have consumed over one million titles."

Lindy mouthed the word "Wow" while thinking about how many books she'd read. Maybe it was in the hundreds. She had a ways to go to be considered well-read.

Tyler was doing the same thing, using his fingers to help him count.

The chief was forgotten since he wasn't going to do

anything for them. His role was no different from theirs, an observer while the political heavyweights duked it out.

"You could give the Delegador something," Mak said softly.

No one replied, but four sets of eyes turned to him.

"Give him all the information you have on the drug ring."

Sahved stood and took the two steps to the cell door. "That is for the Magistrate to share as this is his case. That also seems like something a person involved with the illegal trade would ask about. If we suspected you, you would already be aboard *Wyatt Earp*, answering questions. In any case, we'll begin investigating everything related to you, including public and private accounts, investments, net worth compared with lifetime earnings, and stuff like that. We'll find if you're dirty, which is how you've been coming across ever since we landed."

Tyler raised his eyebrows at the tactical nuke Sahved had dropped on Mak's head.

The chief waved at the guards. "Please wait outside." The two left the cell block without a word, closing and securing the main door after them.

The chief dropped his head and stared at the floor. "I'm embarrassed, not dirty. It hurts me that you'd think I was a dirty cop. I'm embarrassed because I haven't been able to gain any traction on the investigation into how ten million pills made it onto the planet and then into people's pockets. The scale is mind-boggling. How are they doing it?"

Sahved replied, "That's what we were investigating until you stopped us."

"I stopped you when my boss stopped me. His executive

assistant has more pull than I, it appears. That bothers me, especially if his assistant is dirty. When will we know?" Mak didn't expect an answer; it was a rhetorical question. "By the way, I had to release Chloral Mist and her people."

Wyatt Earp, Invisible, Hovering above the Main Detention Center, Batik Magal, Delegor

Ms. Gaster stared at the table in front of her, keeping her hands in her lap. Buster sat closest to the door, blocking her way out of the conference room, but where would she go? He figured it was overkill but necessary to maintain a level of intimidation to further inculcate her feeling of hopelessness. Upon review by higher authority, it wouldn't appear to be coercive.

"We haven't even received our first delivery yet. That is on its way. Maybe tomorrow, maybe later today, depending on what day it is. I've lost track. We already have clearance through Traffic Control."

"Who's 'we?'" Buster knew that Mak had confiscated and destroyed the vast majority of the previous ten million hits on planet. The new distributors would have to get all new product.

"I was approached by a man from a different planet. He offered lots of credits. That wasn't important enough, though. He put me in charge." She stiffened her back and fixed Buster with a serious look. "I run Delegor. The Delegador does what I tell him, but I get no credit. This man, Shekel or something like that? He told me that I would be in charge, and he gave me the name of a person who would handle the front-line distribution. Her name is Chloral

Mist, but she has four who answer directly to her. They would then distribute to four more each and so on until the credits funneled back up. We were given a coin that acted as a conduit to a backdoor finance system the credits would be funneled through a third-party planet. I don't know where it is."

She hung her head. "What's going to happen to me?"

"Since you've cooperated, not as much as if you hadn't. I doubt you would have followed through once you realized what the product was doing to the population. Being in charge is one thing, but overseeing the destruction of your planet is something completely different."

She nodded. "I'm sure you're right. It would have kept me awake at night, but how would I have been able to get out? Once in, I'm sure I was in for life. Then again, I'm a smart person. I would have thought of something."

Buster felt sorry for her. "Criminals don't like people knowing their secrets without them being directly under their control. You are correct in thinking you would have a hard time getting out. We might be able to provide you with an alternative."

"My normal life? All I want is to go back to doing what I was doing, without the illegal stuff. I was good at my job. I was good for Delegor."

Buster sighed. "Only the people of Delegor can answer that. I think I have everything I need. Let's see what it'll take to get you home."

"I'd like that, but…" She paused for a long while. "Will I be safe?"

"That is a good question. We're working to take down this whole organization, all at one time. If we can do what we're trying to, there will be no one left to come after you. What about the Delegador?"

"He'll probably be angry, but he knows that he can't run the planet without me. At least, I think he knows. I have too many of his secrets for him to cast me aside. That wouldn't be in his best interests."

Buster smiled. "It's better not to threaten the man. He seems a bit reactive. He took a bunch of our people hostage and is suing for your return."

She nodded. "What are you going to do?"

"I think we're going to put you on the ground. Like I said, I have everything I need except a little more time. We can't have word of your involvement reach the wrong ears." Buster stood.

"We don't need word of my involvement reaching any ears." Ms. Gaster stood.

Buster guided her toward the door. Clodagh was waiting in the corridor with her husband Alant Cole. "Take us down where you picked us up. Cole, you and your people get into your combat suits in case the Delegador wants a pound of flesh along with Ms. Gaster. Be ready to enter the detention center and pull our people out."

Cole ran for the cargo bay.

Clodagh walked toward the bridge. "We'll make it happen. Give us five minutes. Use the cargo ramp to exit."

Tiny Man Titan raced in and nipped Buster's heel before running off.

"Dogs are usually good judges of character," Ms. Gaster remarked.

"Not that one. He's not a real dog. He just acts like a dog, one that's been dropped on his head too many times."

Titan stopped, faced Buster, barked, and started running at him. Buster took two quick steps toward him. Tiny Man Titan scrabbled away as fast as he could to escape.

"Dog's got issues," Buster said. "Are you ready to go home?"

"More than ready."

"All I ask is that you give us as much time as possible. If you can hold off telling anyone until tomorrow, we'll make that work. Otherwise, this whole thing could unravel. It's across multiple planets and is a complex operation. Please, I implore you."

"What about me being arrested? Am I being let go, or are you going to swoop in and arrest me when I least expect it?"

"That's a little bit dramatic. I am a Magistrate. As such, I have the ability to judge a case, make the ruling, and impart punishment, up to and including capital punishment. Do you understand?"

"You can legally kill me? I didn't know anyone had that ability."

"It's exclusive to the Magistrates. I could arrest your boss, and there's nothing your planet could legally do to interfere with that." He shook his head and waved away further conversation. "My point is that you are granted parole. I need to confirm certain information, but after that, I can commute the sentence, and that will be the end of it."

"I would like to believe you."

"Tell me where I've lied to you or misled you?" Buster countered. "I've only been honest."

She nodded, brow furrowed in thought. "I'll take my chances on Delegor. I'll give you as much time as I can before I tell the Delegador everything."

Buster held out his hand. "Deal."

She shook it.

"Take us in, Clodagh," Buster shouted toward the bridge.

"No need to yell, Magistrate," Clevarious stated.

"I forgot you were there, Clevarious. You have everything you need from the interview?"

"I do. Beau was with us too, for your personal records."

"Hey, Beau. Glad to have you aboard. How am I doing?"

"Great. Seems like you're doing better than when I'm with you. I'm jealous." The SI didn't sound jealous.

"I'll be home in a little while. Keep the ship warm." Buster had been killing time by distracting Ms. Gaster. "I think it's time for you to go home, too. Buy us some time. That will make it easier for us to complete our mission and for you to be safe. Are there any other names you can give us?"

"No." When she looked at him, he saw no duplicity in her eyes. "I do want to say that the Delegador had no idea what was going on. I could have put a lease for the planet in front of him, and he would have signed it. That's probably over. I bet I lost his trust."

She bent down to scratch Floyd behind her small ears. The wombat nuzzled her hand and rubbed against her leg.

"I think you'll earn it back. I'll be in touch." He pointed toward the airlock leading to the cargo bay. When she walked in, the ship was in its final descent. The cargo bay ramp was on its way down. Traffic screeched around the heavy frigate. Four warriors in powered combat armor stood two by two, facing the opening.

Ms. Gaster moved into the middle of them. When *Wyatt Earp* landed, the five stepped out. On the street, the warriors stopped while Ms. Gaster kept going. The Delegador appeared and walked toward her, flanked by bodyguards.

Gaster collapsed into his arms when he was within reach. He helped her into the building. The warriors backed up the cargo ramp, and *Wyatt Earp* took off.

"Next stop, the main detention center," Clodagh announced over the shipwide comm. The warriors remained rooted to the deck, using their magnets to secure themselves.

Wyatt Earp flew the few blocks to the central jail to wait for notification from the Delegador that Rivka's crew had been released.

CHAPTER TWENTY

<u>Main Detention Center, Batik Magal, Delegor</u>

"The executive assistant has been turned over to the Delegador," Dennicron said after she'd heard from Clevarious.

"Time to let us go," Sahved told the guards. "We completed our half of the bargain."

The two guards, who had returned to the cell block, were as stoic as ever. They didn't respond to Sahved's information. Not to confirm. Not to deny. They simply waited.

"Chief Mak Elb Bint! We are to be let go!" Sahved yelled loudly.

Lindy and Tyler slouched on the bed-turned-couch.

"How long until we're free?" Lindy whispered.

"At least an hour. The Delegador has to prove he's got the bigger dangling dino. He'll push it to the edge."

"Clevarious reports that *War Axe* has just assumed orbit and is demanding an immediate audience with the Delegador."

Tyler sat up. "Let me revise my estimate. It's five minutes after Terry Henry Walton makes contact with the Delegador."

"No one is replying to the *War Axe*," Dennicron said. "Terry Henry Walton has given them five minutes before he lands his ship and storms the compound with a battalion of warriors."

"It's like the game is on video, but we can't watch it live because we're on the board. Simple pawns," Tyler said. "I think in the dong-measuring contest, Terry Henry will win. I have no inside knowledge of his man parts, for what it's worth."

Sahved waited by the barred door, trying to catch sight of Mak coming to turn them loose, but nothing happened.

"I fear that Terry Henry will have to land his ship. I hope there is no bloodshed. I don't want someone killed because we are being pawned."

"Used as pawns," Lindy corrected. "Being pawned is different. That means getting passed off to another. It's usually accompanied by a transfer of problems, as in, 'He's your problem now.'"

"Interesting," Sahved mumbled. "We don't want to be someone else's problem. We're Rivka's."

"I recommend that TH not storm the compound," Tyler said softly. "This is already a shitshow with tensions much higher than they need to be. Mak!"

The chief walked in as if he had been summoned. "I am instructed to wait four minutes and then release you."

"How about you release us now, and we take four minutes to walk to the entrance to catch our ride?" Lindy suggested.

"I keep forgetting that you are able to talk to your ship from in here. So odd, that. We'll have to install a dampening field." Mak waved for the holder of the keys.

"Or you could avoid throwing people like us in prison," Dennicron declared.

Once free, the group headed for the stairs instead of the elevator. A clerk hurried up to the chief and whispered in his ear.

"Seems like there's been a change of plan." Mak pointed at the cells.

"No change." Lindy lunged for the chief. He raised his hands, but she was far quicker. She caught an arm and spun him, then caught him in a headlock and put extreme pressure on his throat. He gasped and coughed. "We're fucking leaving."

Tyler walked in front. "You don't want any of this." He gestured with both hands to make way. "Go back to work!"

Sahved loomed in the back of the mini parade, and Dennicron walked beside Lindy and Mak Elb Bint.

Dennicron spoke evenly. "There is a limit to our patience, Mak, and you have exceeded it. Even though you are just taking orders, it would have been easy enough to ignore the countermand and turn us loose. Shame on you for playing the political game. You've made an enemy of the Federation, and worse, you've made an enemy of the Bad Company."

"Launch," Clodagh ordered. The warriors vaulted off the cargo ramp from the hovering *Wyatt Earp* and descended, using their jets to slow them before they impacted the pavement. They still hit hard enough to make an impression.

They clumped heavily toward the entrance to the detention center, railguns menacing the building. The street was clear since crowds weren't allowed to gather near the facility. *Wyatt Earp* decloaked, and a fireball in the upper atmosphere suggested that a ship was entering the atmosphere at a high rate of speed.

Cole had the front right position in the box formation. He gestured for the left pair to go wide and pick up the pace. They bolted toward the entrance, two sets of double doors that were blocked open.

A uniformed officer jumped out to close the door but dove back inside when he caught sight of the approaching warriors. They were too close.

The weapons on hand at the detention center were useless against the Bad Company's powered armor.

Cole ripped the second door off and ducked to get inside. He smashed a plastiglass barrier and stepped into the main reception area. His voice boomed through the building.

"We're here for our people. No one needs to get hurt. Just release our people, who are being held illegally since they have diplomatic protection as members of the Magistrate Corps. Now would be good."

"Sounds like our ride is here," Tyler said.

Mak gurgled and gagged under Lindy's iron hold on his throat.

"You should have listened to your conscience. You'd be less embarrassed," Dennicron added. The group climbed the stairs and stopped at a secondary barrier that secured the basement cells from the reception area.

"Cole!" Tyler shouted and waved.

"Open those doors, or I'll do it for you. Then you can wonder how you're going to fix them." Cole only took two steps across the area before the barrier buzzed and popped open. The four hurried through, dragging the chief with them. When they reached the protection of the warriors, they stopped.

Lindy released the chief. He staggered a step and bent over, gasping for breath. "We have no desire to take you hostage. It was time to leave, and you were the single barrier preventing that. Once removed from the equation, our freedom was inevitable. You have a lot to learn, Mak Elb Bint, about the real use of power."

Tyler bent close and whispered, "And now you have plausible deniability when it comes to answering to the Delegador."

The chief hadn't been playing both sides, but Tyler gave him an out, depending on what the results were of this diplomatic debacle. He could plead either side.

Tyler slapped him on the back and strolled out, flanked by *Wyatt Earp's* Bad Company squad. Once they were outside, they ran toward the street. The heavy frigate had descended just enough for them to vault onto the ramp. The squad jumped on and hurried inside, and Cole closed the bay with a command from his suit. The ship rose and angled skyward.

War Axe hovered at a thousand meters. *Wyatt Earp* slipped under and around it.

Buster waited for the group. "Yeah, sorry about that little snafu." He looked remorseful.

"Back to Blue Heron Four, best possible speed!" Sahved shouted.

"Hear, hear!" Tyler and Lindy cheered.

"Terry Henry is on the comm." Clevarious brought up the screen in the cargo bay. The group mobbed in front of it.

"What the hell kind of Addams Family crime stoppers am I looking at?" Terry boomed through the overhead speakers.

"They started to let us go but then changed their minds," Dennicron said. "Do you know why?"

Terry chewed his lip. His wife Charumati looked over his shoulder. "I do not."

"Maybe someone was trying to extend the standoff?" Buster offered. "Like Ms. Gaster. I asked her to buy us more time."

"That's a pretty crappy way to do it," Terry replied. "We were on our way in. I gave them five minutes. You see, I don't make threats that I'm not willing to carry out. Never bluff with a threat because if they call you on it, you'll lose your credibility for all time. We were coming, and we were going to tear that building apart block by block until we found you. Then we were going to send them a bill for our services."

Terry crossed his arms. He was stating facts, not blustering.

"There might be a drug shipment on its way to arrive today or tomorrow. Any way you can interdict cargo arrivals for me on behalf of the Magistrates?"

Terry looked off-screen and engaged in a brief exchange the team couldn't hear.

"It would help if you had more information. It looks like at least twenty ships an hour are coming through the Gate."

Wyatt Earp accelerated toward the upper atmosphere. *War Axe* followed the heavy frigate.

"Anything else you can give me?" Terry pressed.

Buster shook his head. "I don't think she knew. It was all closely held by someone she called "Shekel." Does that ring a bell?"

"Asheka Burako," Dennicron replied. "He's running the organization that Rivka is trying to penetrate on Blue Heron Four. He was supposed to be a mid-level operator."

"If it's not a coincidence with the name, it suggests that Burako is more of a player than mid-level." Buster waved at Terry Henry. "We need to go to Blue Heron Four right now."

"I guess I'll see you. What about the cargo ships?"

"Stall them. We'll try to get more info. If we aren't able to get you a name, I think we have to let them through. On the other hand, they won't have anyone to deliver them to."

"Mak told us he 'had to' release Chloral Mist and her minions. I heard they still have your gear. I'll try to get it back."

"Thanks, TH. To your first point, Chloral Mist and

three others. That's who Gaster said were the top-level distributors." Buster closed his eyes and sighed. "How to turn a decent investigation into a dog's breakfast. Have we stopped anything?"

The screen went dark as Terry Henry signed off.

"This was all a diversion. We're here going after the peanuts side of the organization." Tyler hammered a fist into his hand. "We need to get back to Rivka!"

Buster nodded. "I understand." He looked at Clodagh but spoke to Clevarious. "Send a message to Mak Elb Bint detailing the conversation and strongly recommending that he re-arrest Chloral Mist. Clodagh, get us out of here."

Clodagh ran out of the cargo bay. Ten seconds later, Kennedy announced that the Gate drive was active.

Next stop, Blue Heron Four.

CHAPTER TWENTY-ONE

Mid-Rise Tower, Baron's Hold, Blue Heron Four

"We got company," Hex growled over his back.

"Take care of it." Ash couldn't be bothered by distractions. That was why he had muscle like the Atchimorian—to provide privacy when he wanted it. He wasn't amused that Hex hadn't simply taken care of it and told him about it later.

Hex closed the door quietly after himself, leaving Rivka and Custer with Asheka Burako, the head of the new mob. Ash played with a stiletto. Rivka wasn't impressed. She could survive nearly any wound he could inflict with the knife, but Custer could not. He wasn't enhanced and had no hope. He could be killed a hundred different ways before he could rise from his chair.

Not that they *could* rise. The carbon-fiber zip-ties were far more robust than anything Rivka had seen before. She thought she could break free of them. The connector was the weak link. She only needed to spin the ties on her wrist until the connector was where she would exert the greatest pressure when she snapped her hands down. They'd need to be in front of her, but she could make that move with a single jump. She thought she could be free in less than a second.

Which left Custer. She could have done this much more easily if she had been alone.

"What is your real name?" Ash asked a second time after railing at her for lying to him.

The mob boss didn't know, which was the only thing that prevented her from acting.

"Tikabow. You are strangely silent for one who has been so verbose in the past. Tell me, who is she?"

Custer looked at Rivka, who stared at him without a tremor or a head shake. She didn't want him to confirm to Burako that she had another name.

"Alberta Finkelstein." He raised his eyebrows and tried to look innocent but came across as someone who was lying but was desperate to be believed.

Ash moved close and hovered the knife over his hand. "One more time, please. Who is she?"

The name "Alberta" escaped his lips, which was all it took. Ash shoved the knife into Custer's leg before he could repeat the last name. Custer screamed with every fiber of his being. Rivka leaned away from the onslaught. Custer broke into sobs, and Burako held Custer's leg down and yanked the knife out. The wound oozed blood.

"Missed the artery." Burako smiled. "Which means you have a lot of flesh left to be carved up before you succumb from your accidental injuries." He looked at Rivka. "How long are you going to let this go on? This is your fault, after all."

Rivka snorted. "I'm sure it's your fault. You were the one who stabbed him. Custer's a big boy. He can speak for himself. I'm Alberta Finkelstein, as much as you don't like it. We're here to help you manage the mob by keeping your people out of law enforcement's spotlight. Stop me when I get to something that interests you. I don't sleep with clients, and if you fire me before you hire me again, I don't sleep with those people either. Un-fucking-tie us, and give that man a bandage."

"Ooh," Burako cooed. "Bluster is *my* game, not yours. You are not Alberta Finkelstein. You're a cop who has something on him and worked your way in. If I simply off you, other cops will come looking." He glanced at the door. "If they haven't already."

Rivka remained silent.

Burako held the knife over Custer's uninjured leg and let it drop point-first. It stuck. He pulled it out before the knife could fall over. Custer renewed his screaming. He stopped only when Burako grabbed his face.

"Man up. The real pain has not yet begun." He grabbed a handful of hair and yanked Custer's head back, then let the knife dangle over the lawyer's eyeball.

Rivka tried to jump, but the zip-ties went around the chair's arms. All she managed to do was fall over, still attached to the chair, her hands securely fastened at the wrists.

"I knew we'd throw down the second I saw your dumb six-legged ass." Red rolled his shoulders and prepared to intercept the charging Atchimorian. Six legs pounded the floor while the humanoid torso leaned forward. Hex's loose shirt covered a chest protector. He made two fists to use as an additional battering ram.

His lower torso looked to be sufficient on its own.

Red knew the only way to survive it was not to get rammed and to avoid being trampled. In hand-to-hand combat, the Atchimorian had more weapons than Red did.

Far more. However, he didn't have Red's knowledge of tactics.

"I beat a fucking poison-spiked creep. I'll beat you," Red called an instant before Hex arrived. Red head-faked one way and dodged the other way.

This wasn't the Atchimorian's first fight, either. He faked one way and went the other as well, but Red was faster. He pressed his thinner self against the wall.

Hex missed the first punch but backhanded Red on the side of his face. His momentum made for a weak strike, though. Red looked for a tail, but this wasn't a horse. Hex had no tail. Red ran after him before he could turn around but stopped short when Hex kicked viciously with his two hind legs while balancing on his four forelegs. He kept kicking as he slowly backed up, with his head turned to watch Red and guide his efforts.

Red looked around for something that might help him. No firefighting axe. No water hose. No door mats. There was a blanket caught in the door to the stairs. He ran toward it, slammed into the door with his shoulder, and came up with the putrid-smelling swath of fabric. He twisted it like a towel to give him a thick rope.

The Atchimorian was still backing toward him.

Red waited.

"That won't help you, Tiny."

"You, too? Everyone wants to call me Tiny. How about I kick you in the nuts so hard you have to waddle out of here?"

"That's funny. I think you're the only one who is going to get jacked up." Hex bounced back and forth across the hall on his forelegs while slowly maneuvering his hind legs toward Red.

Red raised the blanket in front of him, gauging when Hex would be close enough. His legs extended nearly two meters when he kicked.

Hex laughed low and mean. He thought the end was near.

The kick came. Red turned as the foot ripped through the air millimeters from his chest. He dropped the blanket around the leg and twisted it into a loop. He corkscrewed it for all he was worth, but the leg wouldn't break.

Hex bucked, which lifted Red off the floor, but the human held on. When they came down, Red kicked between the Atchimorian's back legs. His foot struck home hard, but he didn't have time for a follow-up. Hex dove forward, yanking his back leg out of Red's blanket weapon.

Red turned and ran down the corridor. He built up speed and lowered his shoulder. The door didn't stand a chance.

Rivka tried to listen to the commotion in the corridor. She could make out Red's voice but not his words. Burako was preoccupied with his impromptu torture. Custer was sobbing, chest heaving so hard he could barely draw breath.

Burako waited for him to settle.

"Just tell me who she is."

"Rivka Anoa! Her name is Rivka Anoa." Custer slumped and continued sobbing.

"That tells me nothing. What is she? Federation cop, maybe?" Burako pressed his advantage. Rivka bunched her legs under her to get the chair on top of her. She thought she might be able to generate sufficient force to drive a chair leg through the mob boss. It was time to take action. There was no reason to continue the act.

"That adds only a little. *What is Anoa?*"

"A Magistrate."

Burako's attention turned to Rivka.

Footsteps pounded toward the door. Rivka could tell it wasn't the Atchimorian. "Let me go, you ball-sucking ass wipe!" she shouted.

The door exploded at Red's impact. He stumbled into the room and then into Burako. The mob boss stumbled toward Rivka.

"Get him! Knife." Rivka tried to get to her feet, but the chair was too awkward on her back.

Red dove for Burako, who spun and plunged the blade toward Red's chest. It sliced through clothing and impacted Red's breastbone, where it stopped. Driving a knife through bone was no easy task and not even possible for the likes of Asheka Burako. Red caught his wrist in both hands to turn him and push him away from the two prisoners.

Burako rolled on top of Red. With an assist from leverage and gravity, Red slammed Burako into the floor and ripped the knife free. Red turned to free Rivka, but the Atchimorian was right there.

His fist clipped Red's chin.

The bodyguard thrust up and cut into a forearm, but the second fist hammered his temple. Red crumpled.

Rivka spun and slammed the chair against the wall. It came apart. For a moment she was free, but her hands were still trapped behind her back. She ran to the side to draw the huge being's attention away from her stunned friend.

Hex watched her circle toward his hindquarters. He danced gingerly to the side, a slight limp betraying the damage Red had done earlier.

Burako stirred.

Red remained down.

Custer was a blubbering mess, and Rivka had her hands behind her back. She darted toward the door but stopped. The Atchimorian jumped into the doorway. With his legs otherwise engaged, Rivka spun. Her foot came around at high speed and connected with Hex's face. His upper torso bowed backward, and he staggered. Rivka jumped and front-kicked him in his upper torso's midsection.

He doubled over, but his six legs dragged him backward. Rivka punted his face, and he fell. Both torsos were limp.

Rivka saw Burako kneeling with the stiletto pressed against Red's throat. Rivka sat on the unconscious Atchimorian to balance while she contorted herself to get her hands in front of her.

"What do I care if you kill a homeless guy?" Rivka examined the chair's seat. Her carbon-fiber bindings had been run through a hook in the back. She stood and slammed it on the table, and the hook shredded her restraints.

She rubbed her wrists for a moment.

"Don't hurt my boy!" an old man yelled from the corridor.

His smell preceded him. Rivka dodged to the other side of the room and stood next to the window.

Burako was watching her, but he glanced at the door. "Father."

"Ash. What are you doing?" Antony stopped outside.

"None of your business, old man." Burako pointed the tip of the knife at him. "You shouldn't be in here."

"Leave these good people alone."

"Can't do that. They crossed me, and that comes at a steep price. You know what it's like to do that, don't you? Maybe you can crawl back to that sewer you call home. Go on."

Red's hand snaked up. He caught Burako by the wrist, clamping it in a grip that belied his size. Burako couldn't move that hand, so he punched Red with his other hand or tried to.

Rivka was on him in a flash. She leveled him with a single heel strike to the face. He tumbled over backward, twisting sideways as he fell since Red continued to hold his wrist.

Red rolled over to remove the stiletto from the man's fingers. Burako hit the floor.

Custer mumbled unintelligibly. Rivka took the knife

from Red to cut the barrister free. He fell over and she caught him, then tossed him over her shoulder.

"What's the egress plan?" Red wondered.

Rivka laid Custer on the small table. His legs dangled over the edge. Rivka cut fabric from Burako's shirt to use as a bandage on Custer's worst injuries.

"I don't have one since we're not leaving him here. We need to take Burako with us. He's too dangerous to leave unguarded, and we suspect he's the head, the one we're looking for. It starts with him. Chaz found the holy grail in the form of the mob's accountants."

"Then we either take him with us, or you deliver capital punishment right here," Red suggested.

"No!" the old man cried and climbed over the Atchimorian to kneel on the floor and cradle his son's head.

"May I introduce Antony Burako, ruined by his son but still trying to protect him?" Red moved to where he could see both Hex and Ash.

"Nice to meet you," Rivka said, then stated the obvious. "You seem down on your luck."

"I've had better days," Antony replied lucidly. "What did you do to my boy?"

"Punched him in the face, which is nothing less than he deserves. I'm going to take him into custody, but I need you not to interfere with that. Your son is a very bad man. Look what he did to my colleague." Rivka pointed at Custer.

"Look what he did to me." The old man stroked his son's hair.

"Red, secure him. We'll head down to the garage and take the limo."

"I like that plan. Going out the front door could have been problematic. This part of town isn't safe." Red looked at the three people who needed to be carried. "What do we do with the Atchimorian?"

"Leave him," Rivka replied. "Where can he go? He's kind of obvious."

She hoisted Custer over her shoulder and stepped on the Atchimorian to get to the corridor. The old man moved aside.

"I told you I'd do my best. Now let us finish our jobs and put him in jail, where you can visit." Red picked up the younger Burako and slung him over his shoulder. He grasped a wrist and an ankle. Red carried the stiletto in his other hand. If the mob boss did anything, Red vowed to stab him in the face.

Not aloud. There was no need to spin up Antony any more than he was.

"I'll send someone for you," Red promised.

"No need." The old man slumped into Custer's chair. "You had to know I'm dying."

"I knew." Red climbed across the unconscious being in the doorway and stood on the other side. "Doesn't mean I have to accept it."

"Such privilege." The old man waved Red away. "Let me die in peace, knowing that my boy is still alive."

"It was nice meeting you, Antony. We can only do what we can do in life. A lot of that is just hanging on for the ride."

"That's not what you did. You drove the train, my friend. Now, go before the denizens are roused."

CHAPTER TWENTY-TWO

<u>Mid-Rise Tower, Baron's Hold, Blue Heron Four</u>

Rivka and Red hurried down the corridor. Rivka pushed the button for the elevator. Red pointed at the stairs.

"Only way to the basement is this way."

Red fished in his pocket and handed Reaper to Rivka.

"You had this, and we still had to fight those two like freaking barbarians?"

"I forgot I had it. My whole focus was beating the shit out of the Atchimorian. You know, to prove I still had it."

"Red, what am I going to do with you after you defied my order?"

The elevator groaned as it started its downward journey.

"I'm not convinced I did anything wrong, but if there's any way you can get this stench off me, I'd greatly appreciate it. By the by, you don't get to go undercover anymore." Red looked back and forth between Custer and Rivka.

"You got that right. I'll probably let you off the hook this one time." She winked at him. "Thanks, Red. I can't imagine what you went through to be at the right place at the right time to help me out."

"You mispronounced 'save my life.' But that's my job. I'd like to think I earned an AGB bonus."

"You earned an AGB bonus."

Burako roused. Red rotated and slammed his head into the doorframe.

The elevator finally reached the garage. The doors opened, and they stepped out. The limo was there, but the driver was nowhere to be seen. Rivka put Custer on the hood and tried to get in, but the vehicle was locked. She made a quick tour of the garage but found no one.

"Damn. Ground floor, then." She put Custer over her shoulder and returned to the elevator. "We'll see if it goes to the first floor for us. When I was with Burako, it wouldn't go anywhere in between."

"The trials and tribulations of hanging with the bad guy. Can't we just take the stairs?"

"They're blocked on this level."

"Bad guy has some paranoia," Red suggested.

Rivka pushed the button for the ground floor, and it stayed lit. "Things are looking up."

They stood with their charges, waiting for the door to open. It took longer than a heartbeat, but they did. Rivka stepped out before the elevator changed its mind.

Chaz, are you there? Rivka tried, but there was no answer. "Did you know Chaz was here too?"

"Here in this building?" Red stood in the corridor close

to the front door. He checked outside for enemies, but there was no one other than the homeless.

"In Blue Heron. You didn't know?"

"Never saw him, and they disabled my comm chip, so I haven't heard from anyone. Sorry."

Rivka looked out the door. "Where do we go once we're out there?"

Red smiled. "There's a grocery store not far away. We can go there. For a few credits, they'll be your best friend."

Magistrate, are you there?

"Would you look at that? A call from beyond," Rivka said aloud before switching to her comm chip. *It's great to hear from you, C. Do you have my signal? We could use a pick-up. Me, Red, Ash Burako, and Custer.*

On our way. Arrival in five. Remain where you are.

Rivka surveyed her surroundings. "They said to wait five. Do we have five minutes?" The homeless started closing in.

Red strolled out. "My friends, gather around."

Rivka's mouth fell open.

They shuffled up one by one but stopped at a respectful distance. When enough were there, Red spoke to them. "We're excising the cancer. He's probably one of the main reasons you're here. In the interim, we'll drop you a couple credit chips. The best thing you can do is not hoard them. Share, and you'll all reap the benefits."

"We thank you for feeding us these last two days," a voice said from the shadows under a hood.

"It's the least I could do," Red replied. "No one deserves the way you guys have to live. We'll pitch something to the planetary leadership. We'll see what we can do. You know me. Believe me when I tell you that I have some influence. I'll do what I can for you."

"We will do what we can." Rivka nodded at the wheezing but unconscious Burako. "Using this man's credits. You all know who he is."

With recognition, they backed away.

"Go your way, now. Someone will come, and I think they'll be driving a food truck." Red offered his hand to shake that of each person present, even though he still had Burako slung over his shoulder. They responded with as much vigor as they could muster.

A *whoosh* and a *thump* signaled *Wyatt Earp*'s arrival. Rivka and Red headed for the street. The cargo ramp descended, and they ran in. All of Rivka's crew was waiting for them.

"This one in the Pod-doc, and that one needs to be locked up tight." Rivka pointed at the two bodies lying on the deck. Tyler recoiled from Red.

Lindy coughed and covered her nose, then ran up to Red and locked him in a fierce hug.

"Let me get cleaned up." He tucked a strand of hair behind her ear.

"Dery said you were going to be tested. A trial by fire. Were you?'

"It was the trial of a thousand kindnesses punctuated by a fight to the death. Yeah. A trial. I passed, though." He smiled.

"Egad." Lindy recoiled, eyes glistening. "You big jerk."

"I know." Red kept his foot on Burako's chest.

Tyler carried Custer to the Pod-doc and put him inside.

He closed the lid and turned the machine loose to repair his cuts and injuries.

Lindy pulled zip-ties from a bulkhead storage area and trussed Burako like a Christmas turkey.

"Red, get cleaned up. Dennicron, where's Chaz?"

"We were hoping he'd be with you," Dennicron replied.

"As Terry Henry always says, hope is a lousy plan. Get the systems fired up and find him!" Rivka headed for the bridge. She made it one step into the corridor when something hit her from beyond, driving her to her knees. Floyd bounced around in front of her.

Rivka swept her into her arms and hurried toward her destination.

Whee! Floyd squealed.

Rivka settled into the captain's chair after she arrived. "C, find me the office of Bankshot McCoy. We go there first."

Tyler appeared. "Custer looked rough. What happened?"

"He was ill-equipped for going head to head with the hardcore criminals. He used to defend them, not face them. He was given a different view, and it didn't sit well with him."

"And the cuts? He'd already broken a leg on this case."

"Ill-equipped," Rivka repeated. "We'll talk more about it later. I need to resolve some things, like getting law enforcement on fifteen planets engaged in rolling up the new mob." She stood. "C, bring up the packet Chaz transmitted."

The information scrolled onto the main screen.

"Look at that line and block. Good work, Chaz!" Rivka

checked the time. It had been almost eight hours since Chaz transmitted the packet, which meant Grainger'd had the information for four hours. "Get me Grainger, please."

"We're scanning the city, pinging Chaz's systems, but we're getting nothing," Clodagh said.

Rivka still had Floyd in her arms.

Missed you, the little girl cried.

"I missed you, too, you big cuddle bug." Rivka couldn't improve on the search for Chaz. She needed to act. She was still amped up from taking down Asheka Burako. It had been uglier than usual, but she was happy with the result. He was in custody.

"Usually, you're far less shmoopy when you call. Usually, you're mean and angry," Grainger said from the screen.

"Did you get the packet Chaz sent?"

"Yes. We've got fifteen planets' worth of law enforcement descending on primary and secondary suspects." He checked the time on his screen. "Those raids started an hour ago and will continue for another hour. I'll let you know how they turned out."

Rivka slouched. "We have Burako in custody. He's in my brig." She tossed her head and grumbled, "That's a little anticlimactic. I feel like you didn't need me at all. Chaz is the hero of this one, but he's missing. We're going to tear Blue Heron apart, looking for him."

Grainger laughed. Then he leaned close to the camera to laugh in Rivka's face. "You cut off the head of the snake. What do you mean we didn't need you? You built the team that not only helped cut off the head of the snake but also gave us information that will hopefully help us to take down this whole organization."

"Chaz is his own man. Chaz deserves the credit. I wasn't kidding when I said we'll tear Blue Heron apart until we find him."

"Chaz. In a SCAMP body, which would never have happened if you hadn't intervened in the case surrounding Federation Station 13. The Singularity exists because of you. The small things can have universal implications, Rivka. In your case, they almost always do." He leaned back and smiled in a friendly way. Not patronizing. Not forced.

Rivka nodded. She was happy to give praise but receiving it always made her uncomfortable.

"Since we're having a casual chat, what did your team do on Delegor? Seems like they're a little bit up in arms. They've contacted Nathan Lowell directly with a protest. The Bad Company showed up and threatened them? I'm curious to hear the whole story."

"You know that I was here, so I'm curious to hear the whole story, too, but I'd rather get it directly from Terry Henry Walton since he has a way of spinning a tale. A very colorful and engaging way."

"I'll request a report from Nathan's office. I expect I'll get a bill, too."

"No weapons were fired in support of this case," Tyler offered helpfully. "Although, one of the suspects on Delegor was killed by a body block from Dennicron. He shouldn't have run."

Rivka shook her head and whispered over her shoulder, "That's not helpful."

"Truth to power!" Tyler blurted. "They made me a

bodyguard. I'm protesting retroactively. I lost your railgun."

"I lost mine, too," Lindy added from the corridor.

Rivka straightened and addressed Grainger on the main screen. "I'm going to have to debrief with my team and get back to you." She smiled innocently.

Grainger laughed again. "I'm sure we can get you more railguns. The only Magistrate in the Federation who has more firepower than many militaries." He scratched his chin and stared into the distance. "I'm not sure we'll brag about that, but it *is* why you get all the hard jobs."

Rivka lost her smile. "Custer's not well. He was kind of tortured, and I think it broke him."

"Kind of?" Grainger looked skeptical.

"He lasted about fifteen minutes before he couldn't take it anymore. He wasn't cut out for this or anything like this. I'm also confident that he'll never take another criminal case. By doing this, he destroyed his business."

"He was representing scumbags and helping keep them out of jail."

Rivka stood. She made to deposit Floyd in the chair, but Tyler gestured that he'd take her. Floyd slipped into his arms and snuggled close to his chest. Rivka took a moment to appreciate the little things that made her happy about her life.

She turned back to the screen. "If he was getting them off, the prosecutors didn't have their shit together. Custer was only using the law. Sometimes the laws protected the perps more than the victims, but isn't the saying that it is better to let nine guilty men go than convict one innocent man?"

"Something like that. The defense and freedom issues are bigger than you or me. I will concede that he didn't go outside the law to help his clients, but I also don't have to like it."

"He knew his clients were dirty, and he even suspected Burako was the head of the whole thing." Rivka crossed her arms and scowled, resurrecting the feeling of being betrayed by her colleague.

"That's probably why he took this case. Take down the big guy without having to share his suspicions, avoiding the issue of hearsay. He made you dig up the truth."

Rivka flopped back into the captain's chair and rotated it to look at her team. They were all there, or everyone but Chaz. She could only see half of Sahved's face because the top of his head was behind the door.

She spun the chair back to find Grainger waving. "I don't have time to yap like a gossipy kid. Got stuff to do. I'll send you a wrap-up report when we know how the other raids turned out. A quarter of them have good results already, and the others are cooperating, all except Delegor. Your team collected the named individuals, and the government let them go. We'll follow up formally from Lance Reynolds' office to slap them in the head and get them to play nice. They've been a pain in the ass since you arrested Bik Tia Nor."

"He was a blood trader. Certified scum." Rivka was less than amused when she remembered that case.

Clodagh interrupted her thoughts. "We're at the offices of Bankshot McCoy."

"Gotta go, Grainger. Need to find Chaz."

"Let me know when you've recovered your missing crewman." Grainger's face faded out.

The main screen changed to show the buildings below them. They hovered over a block of ten- to twenty-story office buildings. Most were square and had little architectural variation. The streets were narrow and precluded a landing.

"Can you put us on top of their building?"

"Of course," Kennedy replied from the pilot's seat.

The ship descended toward the correct rooftop.

"Building schematic, please. What are we getting ourselves into?" Rivka leaned forward as the details of the building came into sharp focus. The fourth floor was highlighted. "Second office away from the elevators, right across from the stairwell. Good position to make a fast escape. C, can you dig into planetary travel data and see if those two are trying to get off Blue Heron Four?"

"I can help with that," Dennicron offered. She stood out of the way, and her unblinking eyes stared to infinity as she committed one hundred percent of her compute power to helping find Chaz and those who interacted with him.

"Can I come along?" It was Buster, who was at the back of the group.

"What if it's a trap? We could lose two Magistrates at one time."

"Nobody is losing any Magistrates," Red bellowed from the corridor, wearing one towel while drying off with another.

Rivka caught a glimpse of him through the crowd. "Would you get dressed!"

"I'm not letting you plan a trip without me. I'm getting

dressed, all right. Anyone named Rivka Anoa who leaves this ship without me is going to be on the receiving end of a tactical nuke."

"Better hurry, then. The express elevator is going down."

"Crap!" Red pounded down the corridor.

"Cole, two warriors armed, ballistic protection. Two in combat suits on standby. Dennicron with me, Red, and Lindy. Sahved and Clevarious, follow up on the takedown of the organization. Dig in and make sure the locals are taking care of business. If you have to stop a ship from leaving a planet because a suspect is on board, don't let anything stand in your way. We'll appreciate any help we can get from the Singularity."

"What about me?" Buster asked.

"Bustamove! I forgot you were here. Sure, come along. We'll have Red and Lindy, and you know what that means."

Buster thought about it, then thought some more. Rivka smiled at her people on her way off the bridge.

"I don't know what that means." Buster made room for Rivka.

"That we'll be safe. We'll kick some hairy buttocks if there are any hairy buttocks that need to be kicked, then we'll all return to *Wyatt Earp* for a huge AGB celebration."

"What if we don't find Chaz?"

"Don't be spewing that bile! We won't return until we have him. Did you think I was kidding when I said we'd tear Blue Heron down in the search for Chaz?" She called over her shoulder, "Clevarious, shut down all traffic to and from the planet on my authority until Chaz is found."

"Consider it done, Magistrate."

"You wield the big hammer effortlessly. I am in awe." Buster followed Rivka toward the cargo bay.

Pounding footsteps told them Red was on his way. He carried Blazer, the last of their initial stock of railguns. Rivka looked pointedly at Lindy's empty hands.

"We asked Terry Henry to get our gear back, including our railguns. I'll borrow one from our squad."

Rivka entered the cargo bay. The others filed in after her. It was like when Mom was gone too long and the pets clung to her upon her return.

"Clevarious thinks the structure isn't sound enough for a landing, so you'll have to jump," Clodagh announced.

Rivka palmed her neutron pulse weapon and looked from one face to another. She stopped at Tyler, who still carried the massive wombat. "Take care of Custer. I'm not sure seeing me will be good for his mental health. I was kind of hard on him."

"Was he a candy-ass down there?" Red asked, shrugging at the poor fit of his protective ballistic vest. He'd lost quite a few centimeters from his chest and a couple from his height.

"Don't say that out loud, Red. I'll say he was ill-suited for this case, nothing more."

The Pod-doc behind Tyler blinked as it continued sending an army of nanocytes to repair the physical injuries to Custer's body. It would take something different to heal his mind. Once the pain was gone, maybe he could reconcile himself with the events of the day. Not being suited to deal with the violence these criminals were able to inflict on other sentient beings didn't make one a candy-ass.

"No. He wasn't a candy-ass, but I treated him like one."

That was enough to silence any contrary opinions.

Cole handed Lindy one of the Bad Company railguns. Russell and Furny wouldn't need their normal-sized weapons since they were wearing their suits. They carried the big guns. Cole hit the button to open the ramp. He and Lewis had drawn the long straws to go down with Rivka.

"All ashore who's going ashore," Clodagh told them.

Red and Lindy went down the ramp and dropped the meter to the roof. They headed in opposite directions to cordon off the area. Next out were Cole and Lewis. Rivka, Dennicron, and Buster walked out together. Next stop, the fourth floor.

CHAPTER TWENTY-THREE

<u>Offices of Bankshot McCoy, Blue Heron</u>

They broke the door down and took the stairs down sixteen flights. No one was bothered, which pleased Rivka. Even Buster did not seem fazed by the exertion.

"Good that you're keeping yourself fit," Rivka told him.

Red was the first to walk through the door on the fourth floor. A sign across the hall declared the offices of Bankshot McCoy. Red thrust his fist in the air. Halt.

There's someone in there, he said. Ankh had reactivated his comm chip.

Let's get their attention. You four head in and secure the office, Rivka replied.

Red bolted through the door opposite the stairs, with Lindy on his heels. Next in were Cole and Lewis.

"You scared the shit out of me!" someone shouted from inside.

"It's secure. We have one individual rifling drawers," Red called.

"I'm packing their stuff. They're moving. I don't know where before you ask. I'm just a transportation consultant. That's a fancy word for manual labor, you brainless goon."

Rivka strolled in.

Red looked like he wanted to hit the guy.

She walked up to the transportation consultant and grabbed his arm. "There was a man in here, not Bankshot or McCoy. Where did he go?"

In his mind, he had a clear vision of Chaz on the floor, half his face torn away. Rivka gripped the man's arm much harder.

"Let go. That hurts."

"Where is he now? The body that was here."

"They said we could have it as payment. A robot man. He's ours. End of story." In his mind, he had an image of Chaz in the back of a moving truck that was being loaded using the ramp at the back of the building.

Launch the backups to the loading dock at the back of the building. Right now. Chaz is in a moving truck.

On our way, Furny replied.

Rivka let go of the man's arm. "He is most assuredly not yours, and if you continue to profess that nonsense, I will arrest you under the laws against trafficking in slaves. You see, that is my friend Chaz, and he's a sentient intelligence. You better hope that he survives. Otherwise, you'll be charged as an accessory to murder."

"Hang on, evil bitch!"

Red rabbit punched him in the side of the head, and he went down.

"Red, please refrain from beating up witnesses during

the questioning process. He's not a perp, just a dumbass, and as we all know, dumbasses say stupid shit."

Buster leaned around Rivka to look at the individual on the floor, who was groaning and holding his head.

"Is this how you do it?" Buster asked.

"Usually. Sometimes we're more active," Rivka replied.

Red frowned. "He should have been more respectful."

"I agree. He should have been, but he wasn't, and we're not going to spend the rest of our days trying to teach people manners. Next time, I'll punch him if he needs to be punched."

"I'd like to say I'm sorry, but I'm really not," Red muttered.

"I know." Rivka pulled the young man to his feet. "Who ordered the pack out, from where, and how did they pay you? You have to be moving it somewhere, so where?"

Furny and Russell ducked on their way out of the cargo bay. Their heads-up displays showed them where the loading ramp was, and they ran toward that side of the building. They stopped to look down before jumping off the side of the building, using their jets to slow their descent.

The vehicle is here, Furny broadcast. *It's starting to move.*

Russell replied to the group, *I'll take care of that.* He aimed carefully before cutting his jets, then dropped the final five stories with nothing slowing him down and crashed through the engine block of the vehicle. He used his jets to extricate himself from the engine compartment while the driver stared wide-eyed.

Furny landed behind the truck, broke the lock on the roll-up door, and raised it. Inside, a myriad of gear was piled haphazardly. Most of it would have been broken during travel, even if they weren't going far. On one side, Chaz's body sat up, looking like an abused ventriloquist's dummy.

I have him, Furny stated. He picked Chaz up and worked his way out of the storage compartment. *I'll need your help, Russell.*

They each grabbed an arm to balance the load before activating their jets and accelerating upward at max power.

"He's heavy," Russell said. "But we don't dare come back without him."

"Nah!" Furny chuckled. "I love stress-testing these suits. We haven't found anything they couldn't do yet."

They lumbered up until they reached the roof, but they couldn't get over the ledge. Furny grabbed it and pulled. He had a solid grip on Chaz. He was almost able to get a leg over, but the suit wasn't flexible enough.

Need a hand, Russell said.

Tyler was the only one in the cargo bay. He ran to where the warriors struggled with the last meter.

"That's it? One meter. Come on!" He could cheer and encourage all he wanted, but that was all they had. Their jets petered out. They weren't made to fly in gravity. They could maneuver in space for extended periods, but within the atmosphere, there was a limit, and they'd hit it.

They both clung to the ledge. Tyler pulled for all he was worth, but it wasn't enough.

"Grab my leg," Russell suggested. "Help it to the ledge."

Tyler reached out but had to hang too far over the edge to reach the boot. His head started to swim, and he got sick to his stomach. He flung himself back to sprawl within the safe confines of the roof.

"I can't do it."

Furny used the comm chip to broadcast their predicament. *We need a lot of help. All hands to the rooftop!*

On our way, Dennicron replied. She left with Cole and Lewis. They bolted up the stairs, the SCAMP quickly outpacing the humans.

She bolted through the ruins of the roof's access door and raced to the ledge, where two armored gloves held on. She saw Chaz an arm's length away.

"Lift him a little closer." They struggled to rise without losing their grip.

Dennicron slipped her fingers under Chaz's chin, then leaned back and pulled, bracing herself against the roof ledge for more leverage. When Chaz was clear, she toppled backward, bringing his body with hers to the roof.

With their other hands free, the two warriors pulled themselves up until they could vault onto the rooftop.

Chaz is secure, Furny reported.

Cole and Lewis appeared after Dennicron threw Chaz over her shoulder and hurried into the ship.

The two suited warriors lagged behind.

"What the hell?" Cole demanded. "You couldn't get back on the roof?"

"Big no joy, boss man," Furny replied. "The jets died on us, which is a lot of bullshit. All three of us could have dropped twenty stories. That would have been no fun."

"Without jets to slow you down, that would have been deadly. Double-check those suits. That shouldn't have happened." Cole jabbed a thumb over his shoulder. "Back downstairs?"

Lewis nodded. "What's sixteen flights of stairs between friends?"

They rushed through the access door and down, taking the steps three at a time in their headlong descent.

When they arrived, they found Rivka standing in the office with her arms crossed. The young man had his face in his hands, and tears rolled down his arms.

"What'd we miss?" Cole asked.

Red put a finger to his lips.

"I usually don't get to see this part. Damn. This looks like the good stuff."

"Shush." Lindy pointed at him with her best mom expression. The warriors were instantly cowed.

"I think that's all we need. Don't leave town. We'll be in touch." Rivka twirled her finger. It was time to go.

"How is Chaz?" Rivka asked.

Cole looked away. "He was in bad shape. Dennicron took him into the ship."

"Security guards did that to him, allegedly. What do you say we go have ourselves a conversation with Building Security?"

The six of them took the stairs to the ground floor, which was where the security office was located.

Rivka knocked on the door. "I'd like to report a crime."

It opened. A hulking figure filled the space beyond.

"Thank our lucky stars!" Rivka cried in a distressed tone. She put her hand on his chest. "Please save me by telling me which of you responded to the situation at Bankshot McCoy's?"

He was one of them. He hadn't been the one to beat Chaz. The other slouched at one of four desks in the office. They were the only two there. Rivka got the impression there had been five total, four from Security. The other two had left with the unnamed fifth individual.

"These two." Rivka pointed and shouldered the door open. A meaty oversized hand reached for her. She leveled a knife-hand strike into the hulking man's throat. He coughed and gasped, and his hands circled his throat as his body begged for air. "You. Tell me where the others went."

"How about, 'Fuck you?'"

Red stopped Rivka from moving forward by gripping her shoulder and pulling her back. "I'll take this one, Magistrate. You can read them their rights while I'm beating this one into next week."

"What are you gonna do, Tiny?"

"Everyone wants to call me Tiny. It's making me angry." Red handed his railgun to Rivka.

The second guard made the mistake of raising a nightstick, thinking he'd make short work of Red by clubbing him in the head.

Red ducked under the raised arm to drive an uppercut into the guard's armpit to dislocate his shoulder.

The guard howled, and the nightstick fell out of his numb fingers. He tried to do something with his other hand, but he wasn't well-practiced with it. His clumsy effort was met with an elbow to his mouth, throwing him back into his chair.

"He's still conscious." Red sounded disappointed.

Rivka took the guard's hand, avoiding the blood streaming from his mouth. "Where did they go?"

Five had left together. Bankshot and McCoy, two guards, and the mystery man. Mid-rise tower in Baron's Hold.

Rivka let go. "They're going to meet with Burako. We better hurry if we're to intercept them before they realize Burako's not in charge anymore."

"Back to the roof!" Cole declared.

"We're going to run to the roof?" Buster asked, looking forlornly at the elevator. "What about those two?"

"Paid lackeys. When they stop getting paid, they'll move on." She gestured at the elevator. "We never take that when stairs are available when in the bad guy's house."

"Is this a bad guy's house? Seems like we've cleared it out."

"Hello. Bankshot McCoy. We have no idea who else is loyal to them, so no. Stair city, baby."

Cole and Lewis set the pace, running up the stairs two at a time. The rest followed, unperturbed by the effort. At the top, Cole was taking deep breaths but Lewis was panting.

"Remedial for you," Rivka told him. "You should be able to run up twenty flights of stairs carrying all your gear without any problem."

"Twice, ma'am?" Lewis wondered.

"Yes, twice if that's what's called for." They jumped to

the cargo ramp. "Red, you lead the parade into the mid-rise tower. I need to check on Chaz."

Red acknowledged the task by staying in the cargo bay. "Clodagh, best possible speed to Burako's lair."

The ship arrowed into the sky and accelerated across town.

CHAPTER TWENTY-FOUR

Wyatt Earp, over Blue Heron, Blue Heron Four

Rivka knew where they would have Chaz: in the Embassy of the Singularity, also known as Ankh's workshop. She went through the hatch. Dennicron, Ankh, and Chrysanthemum stood around the central table where Chaz's SCAMP body lay prone.

"Is Chaz alive?" Rivka asked.

"Very much so," Erasmus replied through Ankh. "He is currently transferring to the ship's system."

"Move over, Bogart!" Chaz said, using the overhead speakers. "Clevarious has turned into a total bed hog."

"What did you see, Chaz? Who did this to your body?"

"A civilian, after they hit me with a million volts of stun power. So many prongs in my body. They overwhelmed my systems, which shut down before any of the electricity could surge into the core of my being. It worked like it was supposed to, I'm quite pleased to say. I'll submit a report to the Singularity on the event shortly."

"Who was this civilian?"

"I fear he's nothing profound. He was on the accountants' lists as a low-level dealer. I matched his picture with the planet-wide database and cross-referenced that with the information in the accountants' database. Before I was taken offline, of course."

"Glad to have you back, Chaz. We can always get you another body, but we cannot get another you."

"You are as sweet as mint julep pie," Chaz drawled.

"Is that a glitch?" Rivka asked.

Dennicron activated her headshake subroutine.

"We need to return to Rorke's Drift. Can I assume we'll be able to go there soon?"

"Soon as we grab three other folks to round out our time on the lovely vacation spot known as Blue Heron Four."

Ankh stared at her. "I have no data suggesting that Blue Heron Four is a vacation spot for anyone. Not even the locals vacation here."

"Sarcasm," Rivka replied. "This place is foul."

"You should know better than to use sarcasm around us. We don't get it." Ankh turned his attention back to Chaz's body. He picked at the pieces of skin lying on the facial structure.

"Erasmus does."

"Yes, he does, but I don't. You should know better."

Rivka bowed her head. "Misters and Mrs. Ambassador."

She left. There was no need to say anything else.

The Magistrate jogged down the corridor, turned at the bridge, and returned to the cargo bay. The ship was hovering over the mid-rise tower. She headed for the ramp, but Tyler jumped in front of her.

"Four warriors, two bodyguards, Sahved, and Buster. They can do this one without you, especially since Red knows that building better than you."

Rivka nodded. "I'll wait for their return." She pointed at the Pod-doc. "Is Custer done cooking?"

"That's one way to put it. I can pop him out of there at any time. Is now a good time?"

Rivka clenched her jaw and nodded. She didn't really know but couldn't see a way forward if she didn't know where they were.

Tyler tapped the controls, and the lid popped open.

Dery flew in and waited, hovering near the chairs they kept near the medical equipment. "Little man! I hope you can help us."

Dery flew closer to her but didn't change his expression.

Custer climbed out. The first thing he did was look at his shredded pants. "So, it wasn't a dream." He stumbled to the closest chair and sat. "I'm sorry. I gave you up to a killer to save myself."

"Anyone would, Custer. Anyone who tells you they can withstand torture has never been tortured, not properly. If you hadn't given him my name, he would have killed you in the hope that I would tell him to save your life, and I would have, so you did nothing wrong. There's nothing you could have done differently."

Custer looked around. "We're on *Wyatt Earp*. How'd we get here?"

"Turns out everyone knew the time that shit was going down. Red joined us after you passed out, and the ship arrived right after that. We have Burako in the brig."

"What about Hex? The Atchimorian?"

"We left him. There was no way to carry his big ass, not that we wanted to. We had you and Ash, and that left us without any extra hands."

"Where are we?"

"We're back at the mid-rise. Our accountants came here to seek refuge after Chaz confronted them. We have him back, too."

"Everyone?"

"We are whole once more, Custer. How about you? How are you feeling?"

"Like shit." He flexed his fingers and stretched.

"You are physically fine," Tyler suggested.

Rivka shook her head just enough for him to notice.

"You asked how I feel. That's how I feel. Is everything going to be an interrogation?"

Rivka didn't reply. His brain had been on the receiving end of too much stimulus. He was not yet able to process it all.

Dery flew in and settled on his leg. Custer jumped as if the wounds were still there. Dery's small hand reached up to touch Custer's face.

Custer held the hand to his face. The two stayed like that for a minute, maybe longer. Heavy steps preceded the team's return to the ship.

"They were outside, and surprise! My people kept them there until we arrived," Red reported. His people. The homeless.

Dery smiled and took his hand away. He flew to his father.

"There's my boy!" Red caught him in a hug, taking care not to injure his wings.

The squad of warriors hauled three people into the cargo bay.

Chaz introduced them. "Bankshot, McCoy, and Rib Au Lein. They need to go away for a long time."

"I'll do just that," Rivka said. "Put them in the brig with Burako. Watch that he doesn't try to snake out. He's a slippery one. The four of them should have plenty to talk about. Monitor all conversations, Chaz. Build our case files against them."

Buster was the last one to board. "That was fun. We'll have to do it again sometime." He shook his head vigorously.

"Your mouth says yes, but your body says no. It can confuse a girl. No wonder you're single."

"I'm single because I'm a million years old. I've been married a bunch of times, but it's not for me." Buster winked.

"Why is it the first time I'm hearing this?"

"Because you aren't prone to gossip, Rivka, and we haven't hung out enough. That includes now since I need to get back to Beau and my ship. I'm sure Grainger already has two other cases to send me on, and before you ask, no, thank you. I'm a white-collar crime kind of Magistrate. I'll be in my room, getting cleaned up. Drop me off someplace good."

He walked away before Rivka could reply.

Custer joined her in watching the cargo hatch close.

"You okay now?" Rivka knew Dery had helped him in

some way. He always did when someone had a troubled mind.

"I'll be fine. My biggest worry is what I will do now. I can't do what I used to do and protect galactic scum from the Justice they deserve."

Rivka smiled. "May I recommend contract law or maybe estate planning? Everyone dies, but few are ready for it."

"People die a little more quickly around you, it seems." Custer threw up his hands and laughed. "I'm kidding, but not really."

"Same old Custer. Jerk." She nodded at the airlock. "We'll drop you and Buster off at Federation Station 7. That's where the Magistrates' headquarters is, but no one goes there anymore. Just Bustamove."

"You Magistrates are weird."

"Get your trash. It won't take us long to get there." Rivka looked at the overhead. "Clevarious, Chaz, take us to Federation Station 7 best possible speed."

"Magistrate!" Red called down the corridor. "I promised my people I'd take care of them."

"Clevarious, buy a food truck's inventory and send it to the mid-rise every day for a month." Rivka looked at Red for confirmation. "Does that take care of it?"

"It does. Then we'll figure out what to do next. Thanks, Magistrate. Any way we can get AGB to celebrate?"

"Of course we're getting AGB to celebrate. We'll send it to Rorke's Drift. We have to get Chaz's body fixed by the pros."

"Back to factory settings, eh, Magistrate?" Red quipped.

Rivka laughed. "Bullseye, Red. That's one of your best

ones yet." She turned serious. "Dery worried that you were undergoing a trial by fire. What do you think he meant by that?"

Red stared at the wall. "I'm nice to my friends but skeptical of strangers. To survive down there, I had to be nice to strangers when no one else was. It was humbling." He made eye contact with her. "The old man was dead when we got there, and Hex was gone."

"C, issue a warrant for the Atchimorian's arrest."

"I kicked him in the balls so hard his grandfoals will walk with a limp." Red beamed with pride.

"I don't know how to respond to that." Dery darted into the corridor, then disappeared. Red ran after him.

Whee! Floyd cried from somewhere out of sight.

Tyler draped an arm over Rivka's shoulders. "Business as usual?"

"The usual. There were no betting lines on this case since we were undercover, but you know what? I like them because they define the parameters within which we operate. It's weird, but I only liked them when they weren't there."

"That's the stuff you think about when you don't have to think about that stuff?" Tyler wondered. "You're weird."

"I'm your kind of weird."

Tyler shook his head. "I'm not weird at all. You know what else I'm not? A bodyguard. Don't make me ever do that again. Me with a railgun? Can you imagine?"

"I hope someone got pictures," Rivka said.

"What about him?" Tyler gestured toward the brig.

Rivka scowled for a moment, then brightened. "C, get our usual order into AGB, giving Christina and Kae our best. Then coordinate a pickup where we can toss these miscreants out the airlock … and into prison transport on Station 7."

"Do you want AGB to meet us at Rorke's Drift after the big drop off?" Clevarious asked.

"That's the plan, C. Then slackers won't be eating our pies."

Tyler chuckled. "Slackers. Like Buster and Custer."

Rivka stopped and pondered the names. "How did we miss the opportunity for a song and dance team?" Rivka looked around trying to decide what she wanted to do. "C, take care of it."

"That's a big sloppy Roger, Rivka," Chaz replied.

"Why do I have two Cs in my ship?" Rivka headed for the bridge. She stopped, turned around, and went to her quarters instead.

"Because you are blessed, clearly," Clevarious replied.

THE END

JUDGE, JURY, & EXECUTIONER, BOOK 18

If you liked this book, please leave a review. I love reviews since they tell other readers that this book is worth their time and money. I hope you feel that way now that you've finished the latest installment. Please drop me a line and let me know you like Rivka's adventures and want them to continue. This is my new favorite series. I hope you agree.

Don't stop now! Keep turning the pages as Craig hits his *Author Notes* with thoughts about this book and the good stuff that happens in the *Kurtherian Gambit* Universe.

Your favorite legal eagle will return in JJE19, TORCH THE SKY!

AUTHOR NOTES - CRAIG MARTELLE

WRITTEN FEBRUARY 2023

"There's cursing, and then there's cursing!" That was a recent review of *You Have Been Judged*, Rivka's first book. It also included the ubiquitous one star. In a nod to this reviewer who will never read anything else I write, I started this book with a Red tirade.

The verbal deluge. The tongue-lashing and smack-down. Much more than lip service.

I canvassed the all-star fans of this series looking for help with names, and you came through! I've had to use a bunch of your offerings. I asked a simple question…

If you would be so kind, please help me with names for these potential characters.

- Big Man on Campus (mob boss)
- Big Man's bodyguard (little boss)

- Woman who tells the above two what to do (real boss)
- Alien with a skin rash
- Alien with six legs
- Red shirt (lackey who will probably die)

First up is Derek Frazer, who offered Ashika (changed to Asheka) Burako, (Ash) as one of the names for this story, and Hex, the six-legged alien. Next up was Tommy "Silver Tongue" Gamble, offered by Mindy Klein. He wasn't a real person, but no one knew that. He plays a major role, like Keyser Söze from *The Usual Suspects*. Chase the ghost who always seems to be one step ahead.

One step ahead because there's a void in the distribution. Resolution. The first four levels are taken down. I didn't think the separate details were as important as Rivka's overall role and the role her team played in bringing Justice to the universe.

As usual, but different this time. An old flame. I wanted to show how relationships change over time. Our memories fail, and we idealize something, deviating farther and farther from reality until it's nothing more than fantasy.

Custer set himself up to fail while Rivka had grown and moved on. There was no coming back for her since she didn't want to go back to a place she'd left behind. She embraced her new skills and, most importantly, the leader she had become and the people who were loyal to her.

Now that I'm back in Fairbanks, we have lots of snow and lots of cold. It's pretty grim out there, but we are getting more sun with each new day. That's the best part of the spring. Sun and warmth are coming.

They're just not here yet. We exist on the knowledge that spring is inevitable. Whether it's three or four months away is the big unknown. We'll wait and watch, just like we do every year.

Until then, lots of stories to tell. Lots of characters to bring to life.

Peace, fellow humans.

Please join my newsletter (craigmartelle.com—please, please, please sign up!), or you can follow me on Facebook.

If you liked this story, you might like some of my other books. You can join my mailing list by dropping by my website craigmartelle.com, or if you have any comments, shoot me a note at craig@craigmartelle.com. I am always happy to hear from people who've read my work. I try to answer every email I receive.

If you liked the story, please write a short review for me on Amazon. I greatly appreciate any kind words; even one or two sentences go a long way. The number of reviews an eBook receives greatly improves how well an eBook does on Amazon.

Amazon—https://www.amazon.com/author/craigmartelle

BookBub—https://www.bookbub.com/authors/craig-martelle

Facebook—www.facebook.com/authorcraigmartelle

In case you missed it before, my web page—https://craigmartelle.com

That's it. Break's over, back to writing the next book.

OTHER SERIES BY CRAIG MARTELLE

 # - available in audio, too

Terry Henry Walton Chronicles (#) (co-written with Michael Anderle)—a post-apocalyptic paranormal adventure

Gateway to the Universe (#) (co-written with Justin Sloan & Michael Anderle)—this book transitions the characters from the Terry Henry Walton Chronicles to the Bad Company

The Bad Company (#) (co-written with Michael Anderle)—a military science fiction space opera

Judge, Jury, & Executioner (#)—a space opera adventure legal thriller

Shadow Vanguard—a Tom Dublin space adventure series

Superdreadnought (#)—an AI military space opera

Metal Legion (#)—a military space opera

The Free Trader (#)—a young adult science fiction action-adventure

Cygnus Space Opera (#)—a young adult space opera (set in the Free Trader universe)

Darklanding (#) (co-written with Scott Moon)—a space western

Mystically Engineered (co-written with Valerie Emerson)—mystics, dragons, & spaceships

Metamorphosis Alpha—stories from the world's first science fiction RPG

The Expanding Universe—science fiction anthologies

Krimson Empire (co-written with Julia Huni)—a galactic race for justice

Zenophobia (#) (co-written with Brad Torgersen)—a space archaeological adventure

Battleship Leviathan (#)– a military sci-fi spectacle published by Aethon Books

Glory (co-written with Ira Heinichen)—hard-hitting military sci-fi

Black Heart of the Dragon God (co-written with Jean Rabe)—a sword & sorcery novel

End Times Alaska (#)—a post-apocalyptic survivalist adventure published by Permuted Press

Nightwalker (a Frank Roderus series)—A post-apocalyptic western adventure

End Days (#) (co-written with E.E. Isherwood)—a post-apocalyptic adventure

Successful Indie Author (#)—a nonfiction series to help self-published authors

Monster Case Files (co-written with Kathryn Hearst)—A Warner twins mystery adventure

Rick Banik (#)—Spy & terrorism action adventure

Ian Bragg Thrillers (#)—a hitman with a conscience

Not Enough (co-written with Eden Wolfe)—A coming of age contemporary fantasy

Published exclusively by Craig Martelle, Inc

<u>**The Dragon's Call**</u> by Angelique Anderson & Craig A. Price, Jr.—an epic fantasy quest

<u>**A Couples Travels**</u>—a nonfiction travel series

<u>**Love-Haight Case Files**</u> by Jean Rabe & Donald J. Bingle—the dead/undead have rights, too, a supernatural legal thriller

<u>**Mischief Maker**</u> by Bruce Nesmith—the creator of Elder Scrolls V: Skyrim brings you Loki in the modern day, staying true to Norse Mythology (not a superhero version)

<u>**Mark of the Assassins**</u> by Landri Johnson—a coming of age fantasy.

For a complete list of Craig's books, stop by his website—https://craigmartelle.com

CONNECT WITH THE AUTHORS

Craig Martelle Social

Website & Newsletter:
http://www.craigmartelle.com

Facebook:
https://www.facebook.com/AuthorCraigMartelle/

Michael Anderle Social

Website: http://lmbpn.com

Email List: http://lmbpn.com/email/

https://www.facebook.com/LMBPNPublishing

https://twitter.com/MichaelAnderle

https://www.instagram.com/lmbpn_publishing/

https://www.bookbub.com/authors/michael-anderle